Jack: A Scottish Outlaw

Highland Outlaws, Volume 1

Lily Baldwin

D1715738

Published by Lily Baldwin, 2021.

JACK: A SCOTTISH OUTLAW

First edition. March 12, 2021.

Written by Lily Baldwin.

To Heather with love

Chapter One

Before King Edward of England sacked Jack MacVie's beloved city of Berwick upon Tweed, Jack had lived a quiet life, setting sail each morning to fish the waters of the North Sea, alongside Quinn, one of his four brothers. Muscles straining, heart pounding, he would haul in the day's catch while the sun shone on his brow and salty breezes filled his lungs. Waves would crash against the ship's hull while gulls cried shrilly, mingling with the never-ceasing music of the sea.

How he missed her song.

Long had it been since he had gripped a sodden net or heard fish slapping their breathless bodies upon the deck, for the English king's merciless deeds had driven him toward a new profession.

Now, he was one of Scotland's secret rebels.

Still, his heartstrings could pluck the ocean's rhythmic sounds, which were harbored deep in his memory, never to be forgotten.

But at that moment, he needed to quiet the waves lapping gently in his mind. Now was not the time for memories. He drew a deep breath, becoming aware of the forest sounds surrounding him.

Hooves pounded the earth in the distance.

Now was the time for action.

Jack shook his head. "I miss being a fisherman." Lowering his black hooded mask over his face, he glanced back at his four brothers. Their horses snorted and stomped at the ground.

"Saints, masks on," he hissed. "Stick to the code. Ye're called by yer saint's name. We are Scottish rebels, not murders. Remember yerselves, lads." Narrowing his eyes to see through the slits in his mask, Jack scanned the ribbon of road beyond the trees. The English noble's carriage they had been tracking careened into view along with half a dozen guards.

Quinn nosed his horse forward, stopping beside Jack. "The hour grows late. They appear to be in a hurry to reach the next village before dark."

Jack stretched his neck to one side and then the other. He took up his reins. "'Tis a pity we'll have to delay them." Kicking his horse in the flanks, he and his brothers surged forward, but then the second youngest, Rory, shot ahead.

"Damn his reckless hide," Jack snapped. "What the devil is wrong with him?"

"He's going to collide with the carriage," Quinn shouted.

Without slowing his horse, Jack dropped the reins and cupped his hands around his mouth, shouting to Rory through the fabric of his mask, "Pull back, St. Thomas." But either Rory did not hear his warning or chose to ignore it. Bending low in his saddle, Jack urged his horse faster to catch his wayward brother, but it was too late. Jack cursed as Rory shot through the trees into the open road straight into the carriage's path. Rory's horse reared up on its hind legs. A shout went up from the carriage driver while the guards whirled to meet Rory's blade.

Another cry from the driver grabbed Jack's attention. The carriage rocked, then listed hard right. The driver pulled back, but the vehicle bounced to the left, the right wheels airborne for an instant, then it toppled onto its side and skidded.

Jack reached the roadside at a gallop and met the guards head on. Steel rang in a harsh clash. Fury swept through him. A guard charged at Jack. He parried, then swung. The flat side of his sword slammed his attacker's forearm. The enemy's blade dropped to the ground.

One guard disarmed.

Jack swung around, his sword carving into a shoulder. Another enemy blade dropped.

One guard maimed.

Sword raised high, he readied for the next assault, but only a cloud of dust stirred. He scanned his brothers—none injured, all had kept their seats. Then he eyed the guards on the ground—none dead. With a grunt of approval, Jack swung down from his horse. His brothers followed.

In the fading light of day, Jack knew they were a terrific sight. They were all large men, and Ian, the youngest brother, at only nineteen stood a hand taller than Jack who was already well over six feet in height. They wore black tunics covered in gleaming black mail, black hose, tall black boots, and black hooded masks, and about their necks hung large wooden crosses.

"St. John," Jack said to Ian. "Secure the guard."

"Aye," Ian answered. With rope in hand, he turned on the guards whose eyes bulged at his approach, clearly terrified by Ian's size. Jack couldn't help the smile that curved his lips at the sight. What the guards didn't know was that despite Ian's towering height and breadth of shoulder, he was as gentle as a lamb—unless provoked. Jack's smile faltered. He needed to stay focused to ensure their mission went swiftly and smoothly. He did not want any unnecessary bloodshed.

Turning to his middle brother, Alec, Jack said, "St. Paul, check the carriage. Make certain no one was injured when it overturned."

With a curt nod, Alec crossed to the toppled carriage.

Next, Jack motioned to Rory. "St. Thomas, gather the weapons." And then to Quinn he said, "St. Augustine, take up collection."

A loud screech drew Jack's attention back to the carriage. "St. Paul," he said to Alec. "What the hell is going on?"

A moment later, Alec pulled a thrashing mass of silk and lace from the carriage. He set the lady on her feet. She screamed and lashed out, her fingers bent into claws. Alec seized her arms, pinning them behind her back.

"St. Paul, release her," Jack ordered.

With a shrug, Alec dropped her hands and stepped back. The lady screeched and shifted her gaze to Jack. "St. Paul, St. John—You are no saints. How dare you make a mockery of what is holy?"

Jack turned his back on her. He was certainly not going to give audience to a selfish noblewoman's ideas of devotion.

At his dismissal, she snarled her fury. "I am Lady Eleanor de Clare. You will feel the full wrath of King Edward. You worthless, Scottish—"

Jack turned and lunged forward, bringing his masked face inches from hers. "I have already felt the full wrath of your King, which is why ye're feeling mine." He closed his eyes, reclaiming his control. He would not take his fury out on a woman. Taking a step back, he looked at Quinn who riffled through one of her trunks. "What has she given to our cause?"

"A handsome bag of coin, but that is all," he answered.

Jack turned back to her. He grasped the wimple she wore. She shrank away as he rubbed the fabric between his fingers. No finer silk had he ever felt. He lifted his gaze to her face. Although he guessed she had as many as five and thirty years, her beauty had yet to fade. He met her cold, blue eyes and reached down, seizing her fingers. Three rings with gems the size of blackberries gleamed even in the dim light. She yanked to pull her hand free, but he grabbed her wrist and held her still while he worked the rings from her fingers. He dropped her hand, and it flew to her throat. Jack reached for her.

"Stay back you Scottish bastard!"

He shoved her hand aside. His fingers made contact with a string of pearls lying on skin as smooth as velvet. His gaze dropped from her neck to her chest, raking across her display of rounded flesh, pressing with her every exhale against the bold cut of her bodice. Then he reached behind her neck, slowly grazing her silken skin, and unclasped the string of pearls. "Scotland thanks ye, my lady."

Jack handed the jewels to Quinn. "Add these to the lot."

Ignoring the lady's insults, his gaze scanned the bound guards with approval. It would be some time before she was able to free one of her men. Then, they would still have their wounds to dress and the carriage to right before her ladyship could be on her way.

Crossing the road, he swung up on his horse. "Saints," he called to his brothers. "Let's ride!"

Like swiftly moving black waves, they barreled deep into the forest, leaving the road behind. Before too long, they would be back at their hideaway where they could rest and ready themselves for the next English noble who rode north into Scotland.

But until then, Jack would be free to imagine that he was once more at sea and the city he loved had never been turned to ash.

Chapter Two

Lady Isabella Redesdale dipped a chunk of soft white bread into a trencher of trout steeped in cream just as her father, Lord David Redesdale, dipped his. Their hands bumped. She looked up and smiled, but her father kept his gaze downcast. She turned away and numbly brought the sodden bread to her lips. She imagined the bread was a stone that would crunch when she bit down. The din would echo throughout the great hall, and for once, she would not have to eat in silence. Soundlessly, the bread diminished and slid down her throat, leaving her mouth as barren as their lifeless home.

It had not always been thus.

Once the Redesdale house had teemed with laughter and a love so bright and strong it warmed the heart of anyone fortunate enough to be welcomed beneath their turreted rooftop. The two-story fortress was part of the once thriving city of Berwick Upon Tweed, but five years ago, all joy had fled her heart, her home, and the entirety of Berwick.

Isabella raised her gaze to the tall windows that ran along the length of the hall. Light poured through. Spring had arrived, but the warmth could not be felt. Warmth, laughter, and love had been shuttered from the Redesdale house the day her father brought home her mother's lifeless body.

Isabella shot to her feet, knocking the table and overturning her cup of ale.

"Are you well, Bella?" her father asked, his voice gravelly from lack of use.

She looked down into his anguished eyes. *No*, she screamed on the inside. *I have been entombed!*

She took a deep breath and slowly sat down again. A servant rushed to wipe the ale before placing a new cup in front of her. "Forgive me, Papa. My thoughts had turned to sorrow. I just wanted it to stop."

She had no more tears. She had cried so many over the past five years, enough to fill the River Tweed. And although her father had stopped crying long ago, he had retreated inside himself, becoming a shadow of the man she once knew.

Isabella gazed out the windows. Once, Berwick had been a thriving market port, the very heart of Scottish export and trade. Merchants had come from faraway lands to sell exotic fabrics, carpets, and spices in the bustling city center. Her own father, whose estates in Northumberland bordered Berwick, had often frequented the Scottish city. It was in Berwick where he first met Isabella's mother, Annunziatta Santospirito, and decided to make the city his permanent residence.

Annunziatta had been the daughter of a wealthy Sicilian merchant. On a clear summer's day, Annunziatta and David had both been strolling amid the market stalls and reached for the same piece of soft Flemish wool. Annunziatta had looked up and found herself gazing into David's pale green eyes. Her heart ignited with love's fire, or so her mother had told Isabella on many occasions. Expecting to face resistance to the match from his own father, David had been surprised when his Sicilian lover was embraced by his parents. Isabella almost smiled, remembering how her father had told the story, recounting that his sire may have been swayed by the substantial size of Annunziatta's dowry. But to David, her money had been of little consequence. They had loved each other; nothing ever mattered more.

Isabella closed her eyes and remembered walking the cobblestone streets with her family amid the bustle of market life. But an instant later, reality cut through the vibrant colors and her memories disappeared beneath a tidal wave of blood and death. She pressed her eyes tight against the images, but she could not escape. Love had once set her mother's heart aflame, but all love and lightness were snuffed out when King Edward of England marched on the Scottish city.

His orders—show no mercy.

Men, women, and children were put to the sword. The streets of the great city had run red with blood. The invasion had turned into a massacre of unimaginable proportions, but it was not only Berwick's Scottish residents who had perished. The Great Hall, a large building dedicated to trade, had been torched, killing hundreds of Flemish merchants. Many English residents had also been slain in the chaos. Her beloved mother had been one of those tragic souls.

On that now distant day, Annunziatta had gone to market while Isabella, Catarina—her older sister, and her father had been occupied in their garden. When the King attacked, David set out to find his beloved wife and bring her home. Meanwhile Isabella, Catarina, and their servants were ordered to remain behind and bar the door.

For two full days and two full nights, Isabella and her sister hid within the solar, forced to listen to the never-ending cries of the dying. Finally, on the third day, her father returned, carrying her mother in his arms.

"I've brought her home." He collapsed to his knees, his eyes heavy with anguish, and all hope fled Isabella's soul as she stared at her mother's gray skin and hollow, unseeing eyes.

Trying to expel the painful memories from her mind, Isabella leaned her head back against the cool stone wall. Her father sat beside her on the bench of the high dais. In front of her, two long tables stretched the length of the hall, but their surfaces were bare. Even the servants could not stomach the gloom and chose instead to take their meals in the kitchen.

"My Lord?"

Isabella looked up as a young serving girl named Mary dipped into a low curtsy. Her flaxen hair was covered by a sheer white veil. She wore a dark green tunic with a cream-colored surcoat. Her blues eyes flashed at Isabella before settling once more on David. Isabella cast her gaze to the side. Her father had not looked up. "What is it, Mary?" she asked at length.

The girl's eyes brightened. "A messenger has arrived sent by your sister."

Isabella jumped to her feet, once more spilling her ale. "Show him in and make haste!" She had not seen Catarina, who had married an English lord with holdings to the north, for three long years.

She turned to her father. "Catarina has sent a messenger!"

He reached out and squeezed her hand. "Prepare yourself, daughter. He could bring ill tidings."

Her smile faltered. "I remember a time when you would urge me to hope for a heart-full and never take for granted a mouthful."

At once, her father's eyes brimmed with tears. He clasped her hand and pressed it to his lips. "I did say that."

She wrapped her arms around his neck, savoring the rare moment of affection. "You did, very often, in fact." She smiled into his pale green eyes so like her own, but before she could draw her next breath, all light faded from his countenance. Despair had returned. A painful knot lodged in her throat as her hands dropped to her sides. His coldness invited fear into her own heart. She closed her eyes and prayed that her sister was, indeed, well.

Catarina had been introduced to Lord Henry Ravensworth during the feast of St. Stephen at Berwick Castle. Within a month's time, he had made an offer for her hand—Catarina's first. Given her sister's celebrated beauty, Isabella could not have guessed why she bade their father accept his offer so quickly. Lord Ravensworth was more than twenty years Catarina's senior, not to mention sour faced and hard. Isabella had begged Catarina to put off Lord Ravensworth's advances, promising that someone better suited to her tastes would come forward with an offer. But when pressed, Catarina declared she loved him, and perhaps she did.

Isabella liked to imagine there was a hidden side to Lord Ravensworth that was kind and attentive, although given his unrelenting scowl, she knew it was doubtful. More than anything, Isabella suspected her sister married to leave Berwick and its legacy of misery behind. Regretfully, that also meant leaving Isabella behind.

Mary came shuffling back into the room. Following behind her was a young man of slim build with brown curls that clung to his sweaty brow. He crossed the hall and stood before the high dais, bowing low at the waist.

Isabella could not wait. "What word have you brought from Catarina? What does my sister say?"

A smile stretched his face wide, showing white, even teeth. "'Tis my great pleasure to share the happiest of tidings. Lord Henry Ravensworth and Lady Catarina Ravensworth have been blessed with their first child, a boy, baptized Nicholas Henry, the heir to Ravensworth Castle."

Isabella clasped her hands together. "A baby!" She turned to her father. He looked dumbstruck. She grabbed his arm. "Father, did you not hear? Catarina has a son!"

Brows raised, he slowly stood. The makings of a smile tugged at his lips. "A son," he whispered.

Laughter bubbled up her throat. She threw her arms around her father's neck. "Papa, we must go to her!"

Her father pulled away. His smile vanished. Shaking his head, he thrust out his hands. "That is not possible."

Her stomach sank. "But Papa...we must!"

"No, Bella." He turned away from her. "I cannot."

Her arms hung helpless at her sides as she watched his cloak of anguish once more wrap around his stooped shoulders. She had lost him again to the cold gray fog of grief.

She steeled her heart and stared at her father's shadow. "May I go?"

He eased back down on the bench and rested his face in his hands. Her shoulders tensed. Surely, he would not deny her.

"Lady Redesdale?"

Isabella swung around to find Mary once more standing in the arched doorway. Behind her stood another man. He had thick gray hair and stern eyes. "Yes, Mary."

"Another messenger, my lady. Sent by Lord Percy."

Her father gasped, drawing her gaze. To her surprise, his nostrils flared, and he narrowed suspicious eyes on the new messenger. Isabella placed a hand on his tense shoulder. His body eased at her touch. She looked down and saw his brow unfurl. After several moments, he shifted his gaze away from Lord Percy's messenger back to the young man still standing in front of them. "What is your name?" he said to the boy.

"Thomas, my lord."

"Thomas, how are our borders? Is it safe enough for travel?"

The young man pulled at the thin whiskers on his chin. "Our borders have been peaceful for some weeks now, but mind you, the journey would not be without some risks—thieves and the like. Still, the distance is fewer than seven leagues."

Lord Redesdale's gaze shifted toward the windows, but he crossed his arm over his chest and patted Isabella's hand still at rest on his shoulder. In a quiet voice he said, "You may go."

She sucked in a sharp breath and clasped her hand over her mouth. Relief eased the tight coils in her stomach. She leaned down and pressed a kiss to his cheek. "Thank you, Papa!"

Someone near the doorway cleared their throat. Isabella turned and locked eyes with Lord Percy's messenger. He scowled, clearly not appreciating having been kept waiting.

She glanced at her father who continued to speak to Thomas, ignoring the other man's displeasure. "Make haste to the kitchen, Thomas. Find William, my manservant. Tell him to begin preparations for Lady Redesdale's journey north. She will depart in two days' time."

Thomas nodded eagerly. "Lady Ravensworth will be most pleased by this news." He turned and bumped headlong into a maid carrying a tray laden with their next course. The wooden dishes clattered to the ground.

"My lord," the other messenger snapped, stepping over the spilled food and overturned bowls. Not waiting for Isabella or her father to grant him leave to speak, he continued. "Lord Percy is concerned that our peaceful borders are making some of the lords complacent. Rumors have spread of talk against the king's campaign deeper north into Scotland."

Fury once more twisted her father's features, but he did not reply.

Clearing his throat, the messenger continued, "Lord Percy hoped that given the unfortunate events surrounding your wife's death that your support would be readily offered."

Isabella's stomach tightened. She glanced down at her father's white knuckles as he gripped the edge of the table. Slowly, David stood, his hands clenched in tight fists. "And why would I offer my support?" His voice grew louder with every word spoken.

A cruel smile twisted the messenger's lips. He appeared to delight in her father's anger. "Because, my lord, the Scottish people killed your wife."

Isabella gasped at the blatant lie.

Moving faster than he had in years, Lord Redesdale stormed around the high dais, his eyes bulging wide. "Get out," he shouted. "Get out of my house!"

The messenger stepped back, slipping on the spilled food. He regained his balance and eyed his soiled shoes with disgust. "Lord Percy will not be pleased."

"Get out," her father yelled. His chest heaved as he labored to breathe. Isabella rushed to her father's side.

The messenger scowled at them. "You would do well to remember that Lord Percy is favored by King Edward. You've been warned." Then he turned on his heel and marched from the hall.

"Papa, are you all right?" Isabella asked as she helped her father back to his seat.

For a moment, David did not speak. He sat stiffly, staring daggers at the door through which Lord Percy's messenger had exited.

"Papa?" She urged him softly, seeking to penetrate his present fury.

Slowly, he shifted his head and met her gaze. He took a deep breath, reached out and squeezed her hand. "Go north to your sister. Set your gaze upon my grandson." His fingers unfurled. Slowly, his hand fell to his lap, leaving hers cold. His shoulders curved forward burdened by the weight of sorrow. "Mayhap like Catarina, he has your mother's eyes."

Isabella swallowed hard as she watched her father's silent retreat into himself. Once more, he appeared ghost-like, a shadow of his former self. Still, she thrust her shoulders back. Inside her chest her heart beat with strength and desire.

"Mary," she called to her servant waiting near the door to the kitchen.

"Yes, my lady," Mary said as she hastened to Isabella's side.

"Please ready my trunk."

Mary's eyes flashed wide. "Forgive me for speaking out of turn, but I wish ye wouldn't go, my lady. The road north is full of bandits and Scottish rebels, and only our Lord in Heaven knows what else."

Isabella's nostrils flared. "I am an English noblewoman, but I grew up in what was once Scotland's great city. I will not be ruled by fear or grief or allow the threat of petty thieves to stop me from meeting my nephew. Please do as I've instructed."

"Yes, my lady," Mary said quickly before turning on her heel and racing down to the kitchens.

Breathless, Isabella sat back in her chair. Her heart pounded in her chest. Despite the strength of her words, fear and doubt coursed through her, but she refused her feelings. She knew she risked meeting danger on the open road, but if she remained where she was, surrounded by naught but misery, her fate would be decided. She would lose all hope, and any inclination for joy or love would fade, until, like her father, only nothingness remained.

In that moment, her choice was clear.

She chose life.

Jumping to her feet, she pressed a kiss to her father's cheek. Then she hastened toward the stairs that would bring her to her chamber. Her future suddenly held countless possibilities, and she needed to be ready to face them all.

Chapter Three

Isabella clasped her father's hand and swallowed the knot in her throat. "Are you certain you wish to remain behind?"

David cupped her cheek. His fingers trembled as did his voice when he spoke. "I'm sorry, Bella. I haven't the heart to leave this place." He lifted his shoulders. "Or mayhap 'tis the will I'm missing." He stepped back, shaking his head. "Tell Catarina that her papa loves her. Tell her that I'm proud of her."

Isabella nodded and swallowed hard. "I will," she assured him. "I promise."

She turned and started down the stairs.

"Bella," her father blurted.

She jerked around mid-step. "Yes, Papa."

"Do take care."

She nodded. "Always."

Turning away, she took another step down.

"Bella," he called again.

Smiling, she turned back once more. "Yes, Papa."

"Come back, won't you?"

Tears stung her eyes, but her smile did not falter. "Always."

He nodded and lifted his hand, giving her a slight wave. Her chest tightened. He appeared so frail in that moment.

"I love you," she said before drawing a deep breath. Then she turned and resolutely started down the stairs only to freeze an instant later when a coach bearing the Trevelyan coat of arms clattered through the gate.

Eyes wide, she met her father's gaze. "Did you notify Hugh of my departure?"

Her father nodded. "William offered to send a messenger, and I consented. It seemed like the proper thing to do at the time. He is your betrothed after all."

Forcing a smile to her face, she nodded. "Of course." Clearing her throat, she continued down the stairs.

The carriage came to a halt. Then the door swung open, and she locked eyes with Lord Hugh Trevelyan.

"Dearest Isabella," he said, his eyes warm with concern. Standing, he clasped her hand, bringing it to his lips. His light brown hair grazed his shoulders, and his fine, blue eyes shone brightly.

She dipped in a low curtsy. "It is good of you to come."

A tentative smile curved his lips. "Of course, dear friend. I only wish I could accompany you, but responsibilities hold me in town for the next fortnight. Are you quite certain your journey cannot wait?"

She shook her head. "I am anxious to see my sister and meet my new nephew."

His lips parted slightly as if he wished to speak. She knew he wanted to ask her to stay, but thankfully he refrained, which came as no surprise. Hugh was not one to force his will on her or anyone else. Kind, gentle, thoughtful, Hugh was a man of great character. She knew she should be elated by the match, but no matter how she tried, she found no joy in the prospect of being his bride.

He squeezed her hand. "I will worry after you, but I understand why you must go."

A smile came unbidden to her lips. "I cannot believe I am to be reunited with Catarina. It feels like a dream."

Smiling, he stepped closer. "I think this trip will be good for you. You will see how content your sister is now that she has wed and started a family."

Bella's smile faltered despite how she tried to hide her discomfort. "I...I hope to find her very happy."

His gaze became earnest. "When we are wed, you will be equally as content." He cupped her cheek tenderly. "Love will grow between us, Bella, and soon we will be the happiest couple in all of Berwick."

"I'm certain ye must be right," she managed to say, although to speak the words pained her very soul.

His eyes shone with hope. "Are not friendship and respect the strongest foundations for any marriage?"

She nodded, pressing her lips together to fight back her tears. She had heard his defense of their forthcoming nuptials time and again.

But I do not love you, her heart screamed.

She glanced over at the carriage where her escort awaited her. "Thank you for coming, Hugh, but I must go now." She hastened toward her guard and allowed the footman to help her into the carriage.

Hugh peered at her through the window. "I know I can make you happy, Bella."

She looked into his warm blue eyes and saw the boy she once knew and remembered a time when she had thought of him as her brother. "I miss the way we were," she said softly. Then she leaned her head back against the smooth, velvet cushion. "I miss the way everything was." Regret gripped her heart as her carriage rolled forward through the gate and into the city.

She gazed out the window at the streets that offered little to cheer her heart after her unexpected encounter with Hugh. No matter where her gaze fell, she was reminded of how dismal life had become. After King Edward had sacked Berwick, his first command was the construction of a massive outer wall. For five years, Isabella had watched the walls climb higher and higher. They blocked the view of the sea and countryside, confining the city—just one more cage for her soul to silently rage against.

Her despair slowly began to fade the further from Berwick and Hugh she rode. Soon, she could see rolling, green hills covered with wildflowers. Shifting in her seat, she upturned her face to the sun. Frustrated, she slid her finger along the rim of her fitted wimple, which entrapped her hair and neck, letting the sun touch only her cheeks. Still, golden heat eased her spirit. She inhaled the fragrant scent of bluebells. A smile suddenly stretched her lips wide. It grew wider still, until her cheeks ached with delight. The rich scents of the land combined with the brightness of light so that she felt as if she were seeing these things for the very first time.

And, in a way, she was.

She had not left Berwick in five years, and the Bella who had journeyed from home before was not the same Bella now riding through the countryside. The other Bella had a mother. The other Bella could never have guessed at the cruelties one man could inflict upon thousands of others.

Sometime later, shadows fell as the road snaked through a thick wood. Once again, she leaned out the window and marveled at the lush green undergrowth that shivered with little forest creatures. Light slanted through the leafy canopy. She breathed deep the moist air.

After a while, her stomach growled. Tearing her gaze away from the passing forest, she leaned down and reached into the basket at her feet for a strip of dried meat. But suddenly, she was thrust back. Fear choked the breath from her body. Gripping the seat, she tried to steady herself, but the carriage continued to jolt and rock. She screamed as a thunderous crack like splintering wood blasted her ears, followed by a mighty thud. An instant later, she slammed forward as the carriage drew to a halt. Wincing, she gripped her aching head, but then she froze.

The clang of swords stung her ears. Someone cried out in agony.

Chest heaving, she fought to breathe only to inhale the haunting iron scent of blood. Swords and twisted faces flashed past her windows.

She was trapped.

She had to get away.

Her heart raced while she fought for the courage to act, and then the door jerked open. A man with hard eyes and a leering smile appeared in front of her. She kicked, lashing out against his grasping hands. She scurried back to the other side of the carriage. The door she leaned upon burst open and she fell. The hard ground stole her breath and she screamed as men descended upon her.

JACK CHARGED THROUGH the woods with his four brothers trailing just behind. They had been tracking the Redesdale carriage for nearly three miles, waiting for the flat landscape to give way to a hill from which they could descend upon their prize. Having at last reached a wooded slope, Jack galloped to the top and signaled for them to don their masks. They had moved ahead of the carriage, but it was almost upon them. He leaned low in his saddle. The thrill of the catch set his heart to race. Moisture beaded against the fabric of his mask as his breath quickened. He raised his fist in the air, preparing his brothers to attack. Once his fist swung down, they would be unleashed like a furious black storm upon the unsuspecting English nobles.

The carriage was almost in position.

Just a short distance to go.

His fist started to descend, but then he froze as a humbly dressed man with sword raised high suddenly burst onto the road in front of the carriage. The driver of the carriage jerked on the reins. Jack watched in stunned silence as the man sprinted to the other side of the road and disappeared in the wood.

"Who's he?" Rory asked.

Jack's gaze followed one of the Redesdale guards who turned his horse and followed after the strange man. "I do not ken," Jack answered absently. Then his fist fell to his lap as another man suddenly appeared, running close to the carriage before darting out of sight.

The carriage swerved.

"What's going on?" Rory blurted.

Before Jack could answer a great crack rent the air. He stared with wide eyes at a tree plunging toward the earth. It fell with a thud in front of the carriage. The driver pulled hard on the reins, but it was too late. The wheels crashed into the tree and splintered into pieces. When he drew his next breath, more than a dozen armed peasants ran out from the woods with swords raised high and attacked his prize.

"Blast!" He threw up his hands and let loose a string of curses.

"Jack, what's our move?" Quinn asked.

Jack shook his head. "We have no move. Those thieves stole our prize."

Rory tore off his mask. His blue eyes shone brightly. "Mayhap they're like us, Scottish rebels. 'Tis as Bishop Lamberton predicted. Our people are once more ready to fight!"

"And look at how well they do against guards on horseback," Ian said eagerly.

Jack shot a glance back at his youngest brother. Ian's long red hair hung in tangled disarray.

"Cover back up, lads. I want a closer look."

Jack eased his horse further down the slope to watch the skirmish. The peasants were, indeed, making surprising progress. Three guards had been slain. He did not doubt that the others would soon be overwhelmed. Leaning forward in his saddle, he eyed the ragged gang. Their humble clothing bore the wear of toil, but their broad shoulders and thick waists belonged to men who did not know scarcity.

Jack shook his head. "Look at their swords. Those aren't the weapons of farmers?"

"What does it matter?" Rory said. "They're fighting the English and winning!"

Jack's eyes narrowed on the scene below. "Something isn't right."

Quinn nodded. "Look at the skill with which they fight."

"They're not peasants," Jack said with certainty.

His brothers fell silent as the last guard was pulled from his horse. Several blades glinted in the sun before the tips were plunged into the wretch's belly.

"'Tis done then," Jack murmured. "Whoever they are, they've won the day,"

He was about to turn away, but then the carriage door opened, and a lady fell to the ground. Veils obscured her face, but the fineness of her tunic bespoke of great wealth. Again, he cursed their luck. Whatever fortune she carried with her should, by rights, be theirs. They had, after all, tracked the carriage for miles.

"I don't like this," Ian said, drawing Jack's gaze.

Jack watched as his youngest brother slid off his horse.

"What are they going to do with her?" Ian asked before moving further down the hill and crouching behind a thick tree. "I can't see her anymore," he called back.

"Ian, 'tis nothing," Jack assured him. "She's in no real danger. Whoever these brigands are, they will not harm her, not when they can ransom her for a sizable fortune. Come along, all of ye. The lady is no longer our affair. We certainly cannot rob her now. We'll have to fill Scotland's coffers on another day."

Jack urged his horse around, but then a sob rent the air. He looked back. Several men were tearing at her clothes. Her scream of terror raked up his spine. "Perhaps I spoke too soon."

"Scottish rebels or not, we cannot allow them to hurt her," Quinn cried.

Rory jumped to the ground. "Jack, we must do something!"

Jack watched as one of the men ripped away the lady's veils. Tears streamed down her cheeks. "Damnation," he cursed when he beheld her wide, terrified eyes.

Ian stood straight. "For the love of God, Jack!"

Jack turned his horse about. "Mount up, lads. We've an English lady to save."

Chapter Four

Isabella screamed while men fought against her biting teeth, flailing legs, and each other to stake claim to what was hers and hers alone—her body and virtue. Fear devoured all thought, only desperation remained. Her vision blurred. Their heaving bodies blended into the thick trees overhead like one hungry claw bearing down upon her, ripping at her tunic, tearing at her soul.

But then the claw shrank away.

Suddenly, beams of sunlight slanting through the forest canopy warmed her face.

Now is your chance, she told herself. *Get up! Run!*

Her limbs were heavy with fear. Wincing, she lifted her head and gasped. Masked men on horseback swung red blades, slaying her attackers. She did not know who they were or where they'd come from, or even whether they were friend or foe. At that moment, the only thing she knew and the only thing that mattered was that she was no longer pinned to the ground. Still, her fear made her legs weak.

Now! It must be now!

Drawing a desperate breath, she gritted her teeth and climbed to her feet. Blades clashed. Men cried out in pain. Blindly, she started toward the trees, but her foot caught on something and she fell. Glancing back at what had slowed her down, her heart seized. Thomas, the young man who had delivered her from her barren home with a message of birth, stared at her with unseeing blue eyes. A pool of blood cradled his head. She squeezed her eyes shut against the horror and forced herself to once more stand. The din of battle blasted her ears as she hitched her tunic high and bolted into the woods.

Having found her stride, at last she took flight, pushing her legs to work harder. She never looked back but kept running, though her side ached and her lungs threatened to burst. But then a sound behind her expelled the wind from her sails. Hooves pounded through the woods, cracking limbs and tearing through the thicket.

"Please," she cried. "No!"

They were closing in on her. The ground shook. She screamed as her toe caught on a thick root. Falling, she flung her arms in front of her face in defense against the approaching ground, but she never felt the hard earth.

Instead, she flew.

A thick arm imprisoned her waist, and, as if she weighed no more than a cloud, she was whisked through the air and tossed over the back of a racing horse. The ground hurried past. With every leap and turn, her stomach lurched. Grunting from the pain, she clung to the saddle's cinch, desperate not to fall. Just when she felt she could bear no more, the horse came to a halt. Still, she clung, too terrified to move. Her heart pounded in her ears.

"Please, no," she whispered as her stomach seized. An instant later bile traveled up her throat, and a gush of vomit spewed from her lips.

"Sweet Jesus and Mary," a deep voice said above her before strong hands gripped her waist and hoisted her off the horse onto her feet. Immediately, her legs gave out.

"ST. AUGUSTINE, HELP me," Jack growled at Quinn as he dropped to his feet and stood beside the trembling lass, his hands hanging limp at his sides.

"Give her something with which to wipe her lips," Quinn urged.

Nodding, Jack seized his tunic and used his dagger to cut off a strip. "Here," he said, offering the lady the piece of cloth.

Still bent over, she lifted her head slightly. They locked eyes. Hers were wide with fear. His protective heart bade him reach out to stroke her back, to tell her everything was going to be all right. She was safe now. But his heart hardened when his fingers grazed the fine silk tunic, and her bejeweled fingers caught his eye.

She was a noble woman.

She lived her life treading on the backs of men like him. More than that, she was English, loyal to a king who had slaughtered his parents and wee sister and destroyed the city of his birth.

"Wipe yer mouth and let's go," he snapped.

She accepted the fabric and did as he bade. His conscience pricked. He could not remember ever having spoken so harshly to a woman. She turned and faced him. He was not prepared for her gentle beauty. Pale green eyes stood out in shocking contrast to rich, olive skin. Her full lips trembled. He eyed her dirty wimple and wondered after the color of her hair. She hurriedly wiped her hands before smoothing the cloth over her gown. Her small pert nose wrinkled with disapproval at her slippers, which were spotted with mud and her own vomit.

Jack shook his head. The lass had been attacked, nearly raped, and, for all intents and purposes, now had been abducted, and she was fretting over her shoes.

High born ladies were all the same—selfish and shallow.

With a derisive snort, he roughly grabbed her by the waist and lifted her back up onto his saddle. Then he swung up behind her.

Rory brought his horse alongside Jack's. "What are we going to do with her?"

Jack took a deep breath, then let the fullness slowly stream from his lips. "I do not ken," he admitted.

Ian drew closer. "We've got to do something, Jack."

"Stick to the bleeding code," Jack snapped at his youngest brother.

"Sorry," Ian said. "I just don't like this."

"Neither do I," Jack agreed. He turned to Quinn. "What are our options?"

Quinn lifted his shoulders. "I do not know, other than for certain we cannot leave her here."

"We could return her to her home," Ian suggested.

Jack rolled his eyes even though he knew the gesture would be missed. "Do ye think we can just ride into Berwick and hand Lord Redesdale his filth-covered princess and ride away once more—no questions asked?"

"Please," the lady blurted, drawing Jack's gaze. "My father will reward you for my return."

Jack watched as her gaze darted from his masked face to each of his brothers'. She trembled in his arms. Once more pity struck his heart only to be absorbed an instant later by a lifetime of prejudice. His compassion dissolved to anger. "Ye're not part of this conversation, Princess."

She leaned away from him. "But you rescued me, didn't you?"

Jack's scowl was hidden behind his mask. "Aye, and before that we were going to rob ye."

Her eyes flashed wide at his confession. "Let me go," she cried. He grabbed her tight, pinning her flailing arms to her sides. "Enough," he admonished. "Lest ye wish to tumble off this horse. The ground is a long way down."

Alec, who not surprisingly, had kept silent until that moment, came forward and handed Jack a strip of cloth.

Jack raised a questioning brow at his brother who was known for his cold indifference but then remembered his mask. "What the hell is this for?"

Alec shrugged. "Blindfold her. Then we ride."

Without waiting for Jack's approval, Alec nudged his horse forward.

The matter had been settled.

"So be it," Jack said, shifting his gaze to the lass once more. "Princess, ye're coming with us."

After tying the cloth over her eyes to ensure Lady Redesdale could not know the location of their secret hideaway, he drove his heel in his horse's flank and clenched his jaw as fresh worries and frustrations blasted his mind.

He had just saved the life of an English lady but in doing so, he put his life and his brothers' lives at greater risk. Now, they were not only thieves and rebels—they were holding an English lady against her will. Despite their good intentions, they had abducted her.

Jack tightened his grip around her trim waist.

"Blast," he muttered, wishing they had waited one more day before setting out on another mission to fill Scotland's coffers. Until that moment, he had robbed unsuspecting English nobles without regret. After all, it was no less than they deserved. They had stolen Scotland's land and were responsible for the death of countless innocents. But now, he was awash in regret.

"Blast," he cursed louder.

He felt her stiffened in his arms, clearly alarmed by the anger in his voice.

Expelling a slow breath, he slowly shook his head at their ill luck. If only he had never set his sights on the carriage emblazoned by the Redesdale coat of arms, then he wouldn't now be trying to decide what to do with the blindfolded English noblewoman trembling with fear in his arms.

Chapter Five

Isabella's heart raced while her bottom lifted off the saddle. For a moment, she felt suspended in air while they presumably leapt over some obstacle in their path, a fallen tree or rock. Inwardly, she cursed the blindfold and the hand gripping her waist but fear staid her tongue. A knot of tears lodged in her throat.

She was so afraid, and so very tired.

Fighting for courage, she tried to remain alert to the surrounding smells and sounds, hopeful they might hold a clue to where she was being taken, but the strong man holding her dominated her other senses.

His breathing, loud and hot in her ear through his mask, muffled bird song and the clomp of the horses' hooves. She could smell his body, rich and woody and not unpleasant. His scent curled around her, wicked with persuasion, beckoning her exhausted body to lean back into his chest and surrender. She shook her head and straightened her spine. As if his scent had somehow penetrated her mind to peek at her thoughts, his hand shifted from her waist to her stomach. His fingers splayed wide and pressed her against his torso, forcing a gasp from her lips. Even through layers of kirtle, tunic, and surcoat, she could feel his muscles shift and move as they rode. Never had she been so intimately acquainted with a man's body.

His hand swept down her hip and for a moment rested on her thigh.

"Don't do that," she blurted and grabbed his hand, jerking it back up to her waist.

"Sorry, Princess," he said behind her.

His husky voice sent a shiver up her spine. Drawing a deep breath, she summoned her courage. "Return me to my father. He will reward you when I tell him of how you saved me from those thieves."

"Those men were not thieves," he said.

His response surprised her. "Of course they were thieves," she replied.

"Nay, Princess." His masked lips brushed her ear. "*We* are thieves."

She gasped.

"Those men," he began, his voice filled with disgust, "were murderers and rapists."

Her hand flew to her throat, suddenly struck by how close she had been to death. "You saved my life."

She heard him sigh. Evidently, he had no wish to be reminded of his good deed.

"Aye," he drawled. "We saved ye, but if ye value yer life at all, ye'll remain silent now until I tell ye to speak."

She stiffened upon hearing his threat. Neither friend nor foe, she did not know who or what he was, but at that moment, she knew he was the reason she was alive.

Her chest tightened. How could this be happening to her? She had been attacked—nearly raped and murdered, and now taken by thieves—when her only wish had been to see her beloved sister.

Her hand dropped listlessly to her lap when she realized the empty significance of her thoughts. After all, her mother had only wanted to go to market, a simple desire that had resulted in her death, and she had been but one of thousands who lost their lives that day.

On any given day, most people did not ask for much.

Few were those who wanted it all and would kill to take it.

Expelling a slow breath, she felt her fatigue overtake her fear. After a while, her heart ceased to race. Her mind became clouded as if in a dream. Surrounded by darkness and the heat of his arms, she finally surrendered to her reluctant savior and leaned back, resting her aching body against his.

JACK'S ARM WRAPPED securely around Lady Redesdale's trim waist as he steered his horse through the labyrinth of tall pine trees. Behind him, he could hear the steady clip of his brothers' horses, snapping branches and rustling through the undergrowth. The ground they trod upon was not worn by travel. In fact, they tried never to take the same path twice when returning to their camp, which was hidden deep within the boundaries of land belonging to Haddington Monastery. They were nearly there, and when they arrived, he would wake the slumbering woman curled against his chest.

Once again, he breathed deep her scent, which penetrated the fabric of his mask. Despite how he tried to remember that she was the enemy, he could not help but savor the feel of her soft curves and the calming evenness of her breath as she slept. Together, their bodies rocked as though one, side to side with the horse's gait. He closed his eyes and for a moment, he was on the ship's deck moving to the rhythm of the waves. When he opened his eyes once more, it was not the vast expanse of ocean that stretched out in front of him. It was a glen, green and lush, and dotted with several small huts. And at its center stood a man of slim build who was clad in monastic robes.

"Good eventide," Jack said quietly to the abbot of Haddington Monastery.

"Good eventide, Saint Peter," Abbot Matthew replied, using Jack's code name. He warily eyed the blindfolded woman resting in Jack's arms. "What have ye got there?"

Jack swung down from his horse, still cradling the Lady Redesdale. She stirred, awoken by the movement and lifted her head. The place where her cheek had rested against his chest became chilled from the sudden loss of warmth.

"Where am I?" she said with a tremulous voice.

"Remain silent," he whispered.

She stiffened in his arms.

Jack shifted his gaze back to the abbot. "'Tis Lady Redesdale," he said quickly, but before he could explain further, the Abbot exclaimed, "Damnation, Jack!"

"For pity's sake, Abbot, what of the code?"

The abbot raked a hand through his thinning brown hair. "Blast the code!"

"The code was yer idea," Jack shot back.

The abbot motioned to the lady still cradled against Jack's chest. "Ye've abducted an English lady. Unless ye're planning on wearing that mask until we can figure out how to get her back over the bleeding border and into her bleeding fortress, then I'm afraid ye've rendered the code useless, St. Peter." The abbot shook his head. "How could ye jeopardize all we've accomplished with this rash move? What are ye trying to prove?"

"We had no choice," Jack said, defending himself and his brothers. "Her carriage was attacked."

Abbot Matthew threw his arms up in the air. "Of course it was attacked. Ye attacked it!"

"Will ye just listen to me?" Jack insisted. "We were trailing her carriage, waiting for the opportune moment, when villains, real ones, rushed the road, killing her guard."

The abbot's eyes flashed wide. "Who were they?"

Jack lifted his shoulders. "We do not ken. In appearance they were peasants, but they fought like trained warriors." He motioned to Quinn. "Bring the sword."

Quinn dismounted and offered one of the attacker's blades for the abbot to examine. "How could a peasant be in possession of such a fine weapon?"

"How indeed?" Abbot Matthew said absently as he ran his fingers down the gleaming blade. He scratched at the faint whiskers dotting his chin. Expelling a slow breath, his gaze settled on the lady who sat stiffly in Jack's arms, her head darting in the direction of whomever spoke.

"Are ye well enough then, Lady Redesdale?" the abbot asked softly.

"I suppose I am," she answered at length.

Jack set her down gently on the ground. "Bind her hands," he told Rory.

"This is madness, Jack," the abbot exclaimed.

Jack whirled around to face the abbot. "They showed her no mercy. I will not speak aloud what they would have done to her had we not intervened. And then what were we to do, Abbot? Leave her out there alone in the woods to fend for herself?"

The abbot blew out a long breath. He looked at Jack. "Forgive me. I should have known yer intentions were honorable." He sighed. "Still, this is no small matter. I will go now and send a message to Bishop Lamberton. He will know how best to proceed." A breeze cut through the forest, ruffling the abbot's long, black robe. "Work out a way to ensure she can't identify ye."

Jack watched the abbot disappear into the forest. Then, he turned back to face his brothers, all still masked. "Ye heard the good abbot, what are we going to do?"

"The solution is simple," Alec said, his voice flat. "Keep her blindfolded and bound." Then he turned and headed toward his hut.

"Nay," Ian said, coming forward. "She will be with us for days, mayhap weeks. That would be cruel."

"Then stick her in the hole," Alec called over his shoulder.

"Ye needn't be so unfeeling," Ian called after him. Then he turned to Jack. "Let me just be clear on this matter. Ye will not put the lady in the hole. I'll not have it!"

"It might actually be the gentlest option," Quinn said, drawing Jack's gaze.

"Quinn," Ian blurted, clearly shocked that he would support Alec's suggestion.

Jack groaned, shaking his head. "Stick to the code."

"Hear me out," Quinn said, continuing. "If she were in the hole, we wouldn't have to keep her blindfolded or bound. We would give her blankets and any other comforts we have in our possession."

"Quinn makes a valid point," Rory chimed in. "Better the hole than to remain blindfolded.

"I'll not hear any more of this," Ian admonished. Then, he turned about on his massive feet and marched toward where the lady sat, rocking nervously, no doubt terrified by their discussion of holes versus blindfolds. Jack's conscience pricked again, but the desire to comfort her was diminished as he eyed the jewels adorning her headdress. She was no humble maid the likes that he knew. She was a spoiled lady who might find improvement if forced to endure a little discomfort.

His gaze shifted back to Ian. Jack was not surprised by his youngest brother's unfailing compassion. His kindness knew no limit, but danger to any man who invited Ian's fury—his temper, once provoked, was a fearsome sight.

Jack watched as Ian dropped to one knee in front of the lass. She visibly tensed, clearly having sensed Ian's presence. To Jack's surprise, Ian unsheathed his dirk. "Ian, what are ye doing?"

"The code," Rory blurted.

"Blast the code," Jack exclaimed, watching Ian nervously.

"I'm putting an end to this debate," Ian answered, reaching for the lady.

She scrambled back when he touched her.

"Hush now, lass," Ian crooned, once again reaching for her. "This will not hurt."

Both Jack and Quinn lunged for Ian as his knife started toward the lady's head, but then, in one quick motion, her blindfold fell away.

ISABELLA BLINKED AGAINST the light as she scurried away from a large, black boot, but its owner followed her. Her gaze traveled from the boot, up a thick, long leg. Corded muscles strained against the owner's fitted hose. Her gaze journeyed further, beyond the impossibly broad chest to the terrifying masked I. She screamed when the giant man squatted in front of her.

"Och, sorry! I forgot." He reached for the top of his head and pulled off the mask.

Her mouth dropped open in shock. She had never been so surprised as she stared up into the smiling, blue eyes of a young man no older than she. He had handsome features, a wide grin, and long, flaming red hair that fell below his chest. She had expected someone menacing, toothless, monstrous even...not a lad.

"Ian, get away from her."

She looked past Ian to one of three masked men standing in front of her. She recognized the voice as belonging to the man with whom she had ridden. The man she had assumed to be the leader named Jack. Ian winked at her. "I'm going to pay for this one." He stood up and backed away.

"Now what do we do?" It was the masked man on her right who spoke. Judging by his voice, she guessed he was the one named Quinn.

The man in the middle cursed before he reached out and yanked the mask off the heads of both men flanking him.

The man on her left flashed her a smile that might have made her knees weak if received at court, but in a primitive camp full of thieves, it made her heart race all the harder. He was mayhap the most gorgeous man she had ever seen with black hair in careless waves to his shoulders and stunning blue eyes. She felt her face warm as his tongue wet his full, sensual lips before he spoke.

"My name is Rory, my lady," he said, his voice husky. He drew closer, and her heart pounded harder still. His beauty was wicked. Thick, black lashes framed his intense gaze. His broad shoulders tapered down to a trim waist. He moved with easy confidence. "I am at yer service." His mouth curved in a sideways smile that made her breath catch. She swallowed hard and tore her gaze away to look at the other unmasked man.

"Quinn, my lady," he said with a bow.

Quinn appeared older than both Ian and Rory but only by a handful of years. His good looks were not as flashy as Rory's, but his rich black hair shone in the sun and his dark eyes scrutinized her with an intelligent air. Within his gaze, she sensed an appreciation for reason and logic, but more than that, his eyes were warm. He radiated quiet, protective strength, which calmed her racing heart. Suddenly feeling greater confidence, she took a deep breath and met the gaze of the man in the middle.

"Princess," he said, his voice dangerously soft.

"Jack," she shot back, demonstrating that she'd been paying attention.

Both Quinn and Rory smiled at her boldness, which fueled her courage still.

Standing tall, she, once more, met Jack's gaze.

"Follow me," he said brusquely before turning and walking toward a thatched hut that stood beneath the shade of a wide oak. Her feet felt rooted to the ground. She had no intention of following the broadly built, masked stranger into the tiny hut where they would be alone, away from Ian, Rory, and Quinn—all with whom she felt safer in that moment.

"Are ye coming?" Jack asked when she did not follow.

She took a step closer to Quinn and shook her head.

"As ye wish, my lady," Jack growled. Then he stormed toward her. If she had sprouted wings, she would have been no less surprised. Lifting her skirt far too high for decorum, she bolted across the small clearing. For three blissful seconds she thought she had escaped; that is, until a hand clamped down on her upper arm. He jerked her around, tossed her over his shoulder, and stormed toward the hut. She lifted her head and looked at the three men who stood idly by, allowing Jack to handle her like a sack of grain.

In that moment, she knew that despite their kindness, their loyalty was to Jack and each other and not to her.

Once inside, he set her on her feet. The room was as poor and rustic as the thatched exterior. She glanced at the pallet and table with two rough-hewn chairs, her gaze lingering on the thick loaf of bread at the center of the table. Taking a deep breath, she turned to face her captor. He still wore his menacing mask. She had to tilt her head back to meet his gaze. He stepped toward her, causing her breath to catch. She backed up several steps, never taking her eyes off him.

He pointed to one of the chairs. "Sit."

She eyed the chair but then shook her head. She wanted to stay poised to flee or to ward off an attack.

"Suit yourself," he breathed out, collapsing in one of the chairs with a heavy sigh. His hand reached over his head and pulled the mask off. Then, he laid his head back against the thatched wall, closing his eyes. His features as were fine as

Rory's but more rugged. Confused by his dismissive air, she did not know what to do or say. Eying the doorway, she wondered if he would notice if she slipped out. Her gaze returned to his upturned face. His black hair hung in tangled waves. Long, thick, black lashes rested on his bronzed cheeks as he continued to close his eyes. She shifted her gaze from his face to the door and took one step in that direction, but his hand shot out, grabbing her forearm. "Ye're not going anywhere, Princess," he drawled, his voice low.

She yanked her hand free and pressed her back against the wall. They locked eyes. Like Quinn, his eyes were dark as the night sky. They were deeply set and intensely watchful yet not unkind. A smile, seemingly sad and pensive, tugged at one corner of his mouth before he turned away from her once more. It was clear he was not ready to deal with her, or mayhap he did not know how. His fatigue was apparent, but she sensed there was more to his meditation. He rubbed his eyes and shook his head. Then he stared transfixed at the wall and his features relaxed as if he gazed at peaceful beauty. She imagined he stared beyond the thatched wall at a conjured meadow or steady sea. And for a moment, she felt connected to him, for she knew that look.

It was the look of a quiet soul in the midst of a world on fire.

Suddenly, the peace of the moment was broken as he reached over his head and grabbed the back of his tunic, yanking it off. Her mouth dropped open as she stared at his bare torso. His wide chest was sprinkled with black hair that thinned into a line down the ridges of his stomach, disappearing beneath the narrow waist of his hose. He stood up, and a gasp tore from her lips. His hose hung low on his hips, leaving little to the imagination. Her mouth ran dry, and her heart fluttered. Never had she glimpsed the masculine physique so closely. In two strides, he crossed the room and opened the lid to a wooden chest, turning his back to her. Her hand covered her mouth smothering a second gasp. The curve of his muscled buttocks was clearly visible beneath his clinging hose.

After pulling on a fresh linen shirt, he turned to face her. Instantly her face warmed when they locked eyes, but he did not acknowledge her embarrassment. Looking away, he returned to the table and took up a hunk of bread. The sight made her stomach growl, betraying her need.

Hunkered low over his meal with both elbows on the table, he took another bite and gestured with the bread to the chair across from him. "Ye're welcome to join me, Princess."

She shook her head. She wanted to eat but dared not go any closer.

"Sit," he snapped. "Eat." His black eyes flashed with anger. The quiet soul had given way to the thief. Her heart quaked. She felt like a mouse cornered by a hungry wolf.

She swallowed hard as she considered her options. Perhaps she could request a change of guardsman. She would much prefer the company of Quinn, Rory, or Ian. But she held her tongue, for there was one man in their number whom she feared even more than Jack.

The man she had yet to meet—the one who gave Jack the blindfold.

The one who wanted to stick her in the hole, whatever that was.

Summoning her courage, she stood tall and met Jack's gaze.

His body was strong and sleek. He smelled like the woods, and exuded power. He was a man used to being obeyed—a dangerous, unpredictable man who was clearly very unhappy that she was there.

In that moment, she decided cooperation was her best defense. Squaring her shoulders, she sat down, fanned out her soiled tunic, and crossed her ankles.

A glint of amusement lit his eyes. Then he gestured to the bread. "Eat," he said again.

Her hand shook as she tore off a piece of bread and took a bite. She could feel the weight of his gaze on her. Sweet Jesus, she wanted to run. But what would happen to the mouse if the wolf caught her?

He looked at her. His eyes started out cold, then flashed with fire. "What's the question biting at yer tongue?"

She jumped a little in her seat but then swallowed her fear. "Are you going to kill me?"

He smiled. And then to her surprise he threw his head back and laughed, showing white, even teeth. Her eyes widened with surprise. She certainly found nothing at all diverting about her question.

"Let me put yer mind to rest, Princess. I have no wish to hurt ye. Earlier today I would have taken yer last coin and all yer bonny jewels, but my brothers and I would never have harmed ye."

"All of those men are your brothers?" she asked, her voice sounded small and soft, unrecognizable to her own ear. She was Lady Redesdale. She too was used to obedience. She sat a little straighter, imbuing her posture with strength she hoped would spread to her whole person.

He nodded in answer.

She took another bite of bread. "Why did you save me?"

He shrugged and looked away.

"Have I wronged you somehow? Or are you merely angry because you did not get your chance to rob me?" She felt her ire rising. She was tired of being afraid, and she would be damned if she was going to explain herself to a common highwayman. She jumped to her feet.

"I demand you return me to my father, or if you wish, you can take me on to my intended destination, my sister's home at Ravensworth Castle."

His countenance remained unchanged. "Ye can keep yer orders to yerself, Princess," he drawled before taking a sip of ale. "As I've said before, ye're not going anywhere for now."

She pulled the rings from her fingers, then set them on the table in front of him. "Take these. 'Tis only the beginning. If it is money you desire, then I assure you, my father will pay handsomely for my return."

"Ye've had my answer," he said flatly.

She scowled, turning away. Sweat had gathered on her brow. The heat and stress of the day were undeniable. She pulled a handkerchief from beneath the cuff of her sleeve and dabbed at beads of sweat cascading down her temples.

His gaze raked over her figure. He shook his head in disapproval. "I'll never ken a noble woman's attire. Ye're suffocating yerself in all that fuss."

"You speak as if I had some say in what I wear." She paused and blatantly passed her gaze over his homespun shirt and hose. "Like your own attire, my dress is befitting my station."

For a moment, a sneer twisted his rugged features. She had pushed too far. He stepped forward, and to her surprise, his face softened. He cupped her cheeks between his rough palms and leaned close. She trembled beneath the warm currents of his breath.

"Why must convention cover a woman's hair?" His fingers slid under the sides of her wimple where it met her cheeks. "It is almost always her greatest beauty." His breath caressed her skin causing her own to catch. He was so close. Before she knew what was happening, he ripped the fabric, exposing her head and neck. Her body betrayed her as a sigh of relief escaped her lips, having been released from her own personal prison.

"What is yer given name?" he asked softly while uncoiling her hair.

"Bella," she breathed. "Is...Isabella."

He laced his fingers through her freed hair.

Did he think her hair her greatest beauty? Her sable brown locks had always seemed plain to her at court—*oh for pity's sake*, she admonished herself. What did it matter? She should have been fighting his presumptuous attention. He was a thief and her abductor.

But also her savior.

Confused, she met his gaze and was struck by the intensity she glimpsed in his black eyes. God's blood, if he had wished to unnerve her, he had succeeded; she felt vulnerable and exposed. His hands dropped to his sides, and he turned his back to her.

Without his gaze holding her captive, her courage returned.

"If you were a gentleman, you would take me home!"

He whirled around and crushed her against him. "Never mistake me for a gentleman, Princess." He pressed a kiss hard to her lips. She pushed against his chest and struggled in protest, but he held her fast.

Then his lips softened. His embrace became tender. She ceased her struggle, lulled by his whispered caress.

An instant later, he tore his lips away.

He was as unpredictable as a summer storm. Without thinking, she drew her hand back and slapped him hard across the face. His head snapped to the side. She held her breath, thinking the end was nigh.

He rubbed his cheek. His lip tugged into a lazy sideways grin. "Ye've gumption, my lady," he said before turning to leave. Then over his shoulder he said, "I like that in a woman."

Chapter Six

Jack stormed from his hut. His mind raced. God's Blood, she was beautiful.

He raked his hand through his hair. But she was the enemy.

He had no business kissing her or pitying her. By God, he had robbed dozens of English nobles. She was no different. Her title belonged to King Edward. Had it not been for the support of his nobles, nobles like her, his cruel hammer would not have possessed the power to thrash Berwick to dust.

No doubt she remained oblivious to her king's cruelty, living within the confines of her gilded cage. The attack against her today had likely been her first taste of suffering. Her smooth, flawless palms had never known toil. She could not imagine the heartache of a world torn asunder or the murder of ones so dearly loved. He closed his eyes against the images that flashed in his mind—a wee lass with a basket of apples, a woman whose laughter had been as warm and rich as her black eyes, a man who had taught Jack self-worth. His parents and youngest sister had perished during the massacre, their bodies buried in one of the mass graves. He shook his head, chasing away the painful images.

Nothing could bring them back.

Quinn caught up to him. "Jack, we have to talk about what we're going to do with the lass."

Jack grabbed a hold of Quinn's shirt, jerking him close. "*We* aren't going to do anything," he hissed. Then he turned, dropping his hands to his sides, and looked pointedly at all his brothers, save Alec who would likely remain in his quarters for the night. "Listen to me, all of ye. Stay away from Bella."

Rory came forward, a smile playing at his lips. "Her name is Bella?"

Hearing her name on Rory's tongue angered Jack, which only served to fuel his ire to new heights. "She isn't yer concern."

Quinn cleared his throat. "It would seem ye've become better acquainted with the lass."

Jack turned and met Quinn's amused gaze. "Wipe that smirk from yer face. I'm not in the mood."

Quinn's expression changed to one of concern. "Ye ken she's a lady, Jack?"

Was his attraction to her so transparent? "What of it?" Jack growled.

"Well, 'tis just that ye're a commoner," Quinn answered.

"And a rebel," Rory chimed in.

"Not to mention a thief," Ian added.

Jack shrugged. "We're all commoners and rebels."

"Aye," Quinn said. "But ye seem to be the only one forgetting it."

"I've forgotten nothing. She's the enemy," Jack hissed before turning on his heel.

"Where are ye going?" Quinn called after him.

"To talk to Rose. The Princess needs a change of clothes."

"Och, if Rose hears wind of there being another female in camp, she's going to declare a feast day and throw a party," Rory called out, laughing.

"She'll have yer hide if she finds out you supported Alec's idea of throwing her in the hole," Jack shot back.

"It wasn't my idea!"

"True, but one expects that sort of thing from Alec."

Jack wove his way down the path that led to his sister's hut, which was deeper in the woods, providing her with privacy from her five younger brothers.

When he stepped into the small clearing, he spied her standing beside the fire, adding some scraps to a hanging pot.

"'Tis high time ye came by to show me yer body still in one piece," she said, disapprovingly.

Jack leaned down and placed a kiss on Rose's cheek. Her red hair was pulled away from her face, and her kind blue eyes smiled up at him. She and Ian resembled their father while the rest of them took after their mother with their black hair.

Rose scrutinized his face. "Whatever ye're brooding about stop it, ye hear? Now, why don't ye sit down, eat some pottage, and ye can tell me all about the lass ye abducted."

Jack swore under his breath for which he received a cuff upside his head. "Rose, could we have one visit where ye don't beat the hell out of me for once." He pretended to look cross, then gave her a pinch around the middle that bent her over with laughter. Rose's two weaknesses were easy to exploit. She was extremely ticklish and a champion for anyone or anything she deemed as weaker.

"Who told ye?" Jack asked after she handed him a bowl of thick stew. "Let me venture a guess, Ian?"

"Nay, 'twas Rory. He told me about her fine looks." Her smile vanished. She stopped stirring the pottage and pointed her spoon at him. "Ye listen to me, Jack MacVie. Ye keep Rory away from the poor lass. Ye know what he'll do. Love her and leave her, he will."

An image of Rory plying Isabella with his charms flitted through Jack's mind. He put down his bowl.

"What's the matter with my stew?" Rose asked, scowling.

"'Tis delicious, but I've no appetite suddenly." He leaned forward in his seat. "Trust me. Rory will not lay a finger on her unless he's interested in losing one."

Rose clucked her approval. "See that he doesn't."

Jack stood. "I need to borrow one of yer tunics."

Rose scrutinized his form from head to toe, then shook her head. "Nay, it won't suit ye." She laughed heartily. "'Twas only a jest. I ken it is for the lady. Wait here," she said before disappearing inside her hut. She emerged moments later with what Jack recognized as her finest tunic and surcoat, reserved for their yearly sojourn to Inverness.

Jack shook his head. "Absolutely not."

"Rory said she is the daughter of Lord Redesdale. She is accustomed to finery. We should try to make her feel at home."

Jack grabbed the violet silk tunic from Rose's hand. An image of Isabella clad in the soft gown with her olive skin and pale green eyes stirred his desire. Despite being dirt smeared, she had smelled like an angel. He closed his eyes and felt the curve of her lips yielding to his own. She had tasted of honey.

Opening his eyes, he shook his head. "Nay, absolutely not." He stormed inside Rose's hut, determined to find something that might dimmish not enhance their captive's beauty. Anyway, he had no intention of pampering his princess. It would be good for her to taste life's meager offerings. Jack flipped open Rose's chest and shuffled through the clothing until he came across a stained, threadbare woolen tunic. "This will do nicely."

"Nay! That is my oldest work dress. I only wear it when the task is truly filthy, like cleaning out the animal pens."

"Perfect," Jack said, walking past her and stepping outside.

"What has the lass ever done to ye?" Rose called after him.

He ignored both her question and the scolding tone in her voice. He owed the lady nothing—he had already saved her life, which he was certain she would soon forget. Noble ladies were all narcissistic creatures—puddles had greater depth.

Then why had he kissed her?

He thought back to that moment in his hut. She had been standing before him, willing herself to appear brave and resolute despite how terrified she must have been. She had thrust out her chin, putting her full lips on display. Then she had made that quip about him not being a gentleman. She had practically dared him to kiss her, and now that she had had time to ruminate on his ungentlemanly advance, he was certain to hear all about his uncouth manners and inferior station.

Ready for battle, he stormed inside his hut, but the scene that awaited him could not have been more surprising. She was asleep, lying on his pallet, and despite the warmth of the day, wrapped tightly in his blanket. With great care to be silent, he laid the bundle of clean but worn clothing beside her, lit a candle against the advancing shadow, and sat down at the table and watched her sleep.

After an hour passed, she began to stir. Her lashes fluttered against her cheeks, which had been warmed pink by the fire. She opened her eyes and straightaway spied the bundle he had left her. Sitting up, she unfolded the tunic and smiled. He had expected disdain. She was supposed to turn her nose up at the crude garments, not delight in them as though they were made of the finest silk. She smiled, smelling the clean fabric. He leaned in, drawn by her pleasure, but his movement caught her eye. To his surprise, she held up the tunic and dipped her head. "Thank you for this."

Not knowing how to respond, he gave her a curt nod. "I will leave you to dress. When ye're finished, come join my family by the fire, Princess." This time it had been a struggle to lace his words with malice.

"Wait," she said.

He turned around and gave her an expectant look.

"Will yer other brother be there?" she asked, wringing her hands.

Was she excited? Nervous?

His shoulders tensed. "I have several brothers. Ye'll have to be more specific."

"The one who wanted to stick me in the hole."

Jack's shoulders eased. "Ye needn't fear Alec. Anyway, he usually keeps to himself."

He started to turn away, but then he stopped and looked back. "To put yer mind at ease, once and for all, ye're safe here. I will protect ye."

He turned away, refusing the sudden desire to graze the backs of his fingers down her silken cheek. As he stepped out into the evening air, he was grateful for the slight chill, although it was hardly enough to quell his burgeoning desire?

ISABELLA RAN HER FINGERS through her hair, working out most of the snarls. With nothing to tie it up, she swept her hair from her shoulders, letting it fall free down her back. She had not intended to sleep when she had laid down on Jack's pallet, only to cease the spinning in her head. But her body took for itself what it needed, and now she felt all the better having rested.

She smoothed her hands over the soft, worn fabric of her borrowed tunic. It had caressed her curves like a whisper when she pulled it on. Smiling, she closed her eyes and savored the unusual feeling of being unbound. Her own clothing was designed to contain and restrict, but now she could move and breathe and feel.

She longed to step outside, to invite the night air on her neck and shoulders, but she hesitated when she stood in front of the door. Jack had promised that she was safe—but could she trust a thief?

Her fingertips touched her lips, still swollen from his hard kiss. He was nothing like the men at court, nothing like Hugh. Hugh's slim build and soft hands seemed childlike now that she had felt Jack's hard strength.

She had sense enough to fear him. But fear alone had not set her heart to race when he drew near. His smell, his rough hands, and deep voice excited her, and the quietness she had glimpsed in him kept her wondering about the real man beneath the mask.

She shook her head at herself, feeling betrayed by her own thoughts. Taken as a whole, his behavior toward her had been hostile. Confused, she clenched and unclenched her fists as she continued to stare at the door.

He was a thief. They were all thieves, and she their captive.

"Enough," she said out loud.

All she truly knew for certain was that she was tired and hungrier than she could ever remember being.

With a deep breath, she pushed the door open and stepped out into the cool night. Closing her eyes, she deeply inhaled the scents of cooked meat and herbs. Her stomach growled. She looked toward the fire. Four sets of male eyes stared at her. She self-consciously ran her hand over her free-flowing hair.

Ian dashed toward her. "Lady Redesdale, I'm so glad ye've joined us."

"Good evening," she replied awkwardly, meeting Ian's kind gaze.

Were they her abductors or saviors?

Rory stood. "My lady," he said, taking her hand. She blushed when he kissed her hand. Damn his eyes. He was more beautiful than any man should ever be.

She was relieved when Quinn stepped forward. "Come," he said, offering her his arm. "Ye must sample the stew our sister, Rose, has made."

Isabella's heart skipped with relief when she noticed the woman sitting on a log by the fire. She was trim with a beautiful smile and thick, curly red hair that fell to her waist. She must have been near thirty and was as lovely as the flower for which she'd been named.

Isabella dipped in a low curtsy in front of Rose. "Forgive me. I did not mean to disturb your meal."

"Och, sweetling, ye've done nothing wrong, lass. I'm delighted ye're here." Rose patted the log next to her. Isabella sat and looked across the flames. Jack's eyes bore into hers.

"Jack MacVie, turn yer gaze elsewhere. Can't ye tell yer making her nervous? Nay, in fact, eat yer supper, all of ye." Rose stood and offered Isabella her hand. "The lady and I are going to sit over there."

Brows drawn in a deep frown, Jack started to stand, but whether to voice his protest or follow after, Isabella knew naught. Either way, Rose gave him no quarter.

"Ye just sit back down, Jack," she snapped.

Isabella's eyes widened. She stood and hastened after Rose. It would seem she had misjudged Jack as the leader. Clearly, Rose was in charge.

"I cannot imagine anyone talking to Jack that way," Isabella whispered when she drew alongside Rose.

"I am three years Jack's senior. The eldest MacVie, and I make sure that none of my wee brothers forget it."

Isabella could not suppress her smile. "I would not call any one of them wee."

Rose sat beneath a large oak. Isabella joined her, leaning her back against the cool trunk. "This is better. Thank you, Rose."

Rose smiled and handed her a bowl. "Hush now, my lady, and have some stew. Ye must be famished."

Isabella gladly accepted the wooden bowl. The stew was thick with chunks of rabbit and tasted of Rosemary and garlic. "This is delicious."

"As hungry as ye must be, my lady, I'd wager even the poorest fare would be pleasing to yer palate."

Isabella smiled. "Believe me or not, Rose, but this is very fine."

Rose surprised Isabella by blushing. "Thank ye, my lady."

They sat in comfortable silence while Isabella finished her stew. She soaked up the last of it with a thick bannock. It had been a simple but truly satisfying meal. She almost felt like herself again. But then she glanced across the camp at the fire. Jack's gaze was still on her, his face impossible to read. She looked away, unable to withstand the intensity of his gaze. She looked to Rose for distraction.

"Are ye married?" Isabella asked.

Rose cast her gaze downward and shook her head. "My husband and three daughters were killed during the massacre."

Isabella's hand flew to her lips. "Oh, Rose, I am so sorry."

Rose raised her eyes, which glistened with unshed tears. "'Tis done. Naught can bring them back. Some days are harder than others." Her voice cracked. "There are mornings when I wake, and I must force myself to breathe and command my feet to walk. Those are my hollow days. And then, there are days when I taste joy." Her lips lifted in a sideways smile not unlike Jack's. "Just a taste, mind, but those are good days."

Isabella swallowed the knot that had formed in her throat. "By the grace of God," she whispered.

Rose nodded and patted Isabella's leg. "Ye're right about that. Anyway, most days leave little time for remembering. I've got my brothers to care for, and they are good to me."

Isabella lifted a skeptical brow. How good could a pack of thieves be?

"I ken what ye're thinking, but ye're wrong. They are all good and decent men. Quinn, who is six and twenty, is just two years younger than Jack. He is the best of us, to be sure. He has a head for learning. The monks have taught him how to read and write. He can do his numbers, and he speaks Latin and French. His patience seldom runs out. I've told him time and again to take his vows and join the monastery, but like, the rest of my brothers, he has a great appreciation for the fairer sex."

Isabella arched a brow at her. "I cannot imagine any of them as men of the cloth, least of all Rory."

Rose chuckled. "At two and twenty, he is the second youngest. And I swear to ye, he's been seducing women since the cradle. The attention he received as a baby was more than ye can imagine. Never could a woman walk by him and not ooh and ahhh. He didn't learn to walk until he was near two. He never had to. He spent most of his time in his favorite place—asleep with a bosom for a pillow. Too pretty for his own good, Rory is."

"His lashes would be the envy of every lady at court."

Rose threw her head back and her laughter rang out, easing Isabella's spirit.

"And then, of course, there's Ian. He's the baby."

Isabella could not hold back a chuckle. "Baby? You can imagine my terror when I first saw Ian, the giant, with his horrible black mask. But can ye imagine my even greater surprise when he took it off, and the lion was no more than a lamb."

"A lamb to be sure; well, if a lamb also had a deadly aim and a fierce side the likes of which ye would not believe."

"I cannot imagine his countenance in any other way than happy."

"He is that, most of the time. But push him to anger and his temper flares. 'Tis the red hair." She winked, lifting a lock of her own strawberry curls. "Oh, and what a voice he has. I tell ye, he sings like an angel. He's just nineteen. His red hair and sky-blue eyes were a blessing from our mother, but his size is all da."

"It would seem your father was a large and handsome man," Isabella observed.

"Aye, that he was."

"Forgive me, Rose, but you missed one brother? The one most eager to throw me into the hole."

"Och, for pity's sake! That would be Alec."

"What is he like?" Isabella asked, her curiosity overtaking her fear.

"Alec is four and twenty. And do not be mistaken, my lady, I highly doubt Alec would have been eager to throw you in the hole."

"He's a true saint," Isabella said, unable to keep the sarcasm from her voice. "Sorry," she muttered.

"I ken Jack is keeping ye here against yer will. Ye're entitled to yer displeasure. But, in truth, Alec is neither a saint nor a sinner. He's hard to understand." Rose paused, then with a sigh, she said, "I'm sorry, lass. I know it must sound like I'm making excuses for him. 'Tis just that I have a special place in my heart for Alec. He was always an odd sort of lad. He has the sight, ye ken, and knows all manner of things before they happen. In fact, the day before King Edward attacked Berwick, my husband and daughters had taken ill. I had no bayberry to bring down their fevers, so I enlisted the aid of my youngest brothers. On the next day, Alec was supposed to join us in the woods near the city to forage for herbs, but when the time came to leave, he refused. He said that during the night he had dreamt the world was on fire, then went to the kirk to pray. When Edward attacked, Ian, Rory, and I were safe in the woods, but Alec remained in the city and witnessed it all. 'Tis a miracle he's alive."

Knowing that Alec had the sight did little to ease her fear of him, despite piquing her curiosity. Still, she decided to forgo asking questions about the middle MacVie brother and instead asked, "What about Jack and Quinn? Where were they when the king attacked?"

"Once upon a time, Jack and Quinn were fishermen. They were at sea when Berwick's defenses fell." A shadow of pain flitted across Rose's face, but then she cleared her throat and brightened her sad eyes. "Right. Enough sad talk. And I'll spare ye my account of Jack. I figure ye've learned enough about him already."

Isabella's thoughts wandered straight back to Jack's kiss. Did Rose know how acquainted they had become? Isabella hid her blush by busying herself with stacking the dirty bowls. She felt a nervous jump in her belly.

Rose stood, dusting off her hands. "Now that ye ken a little more about my younger brothers, are ye ready to rejoin their company?"

Hearing Rose's account of the MacVie brothers had eased some of her discomfort, although she was just as confused as ever. "Will ye steal me away again if my nerves get the better of me?"

Rose smiled. "They're not the only thieves in the family."

Bella knew Rose was only jesting. Still, the reminder set her heart to race once more as she followed her back to sit by the fire with her handsome captors.

Chapter Seven

In the beginning, Isabella felt awkward and nervous surrounded by the MacVie siblings beneath a blanket of stars. But after a while, she forgot the confusing circumstances for being there, and instead found herself delighting in their company. For so long she had felt imprisoned within her lonely fortress, and now, despite being an actual captive, she felt freer than she had in years. It was clear that they loved each other. Laughter filled the night, and her heart. And in that moment, she remembered what it felt like to have a family.

Listening to Rory recount a particularly funny tale of the first time Ian had been mistaken for a full-grown man when he was naught but one and ten, she bent over with laughter. But when she sat straight, she locked eyes with Jack whose intense gaze made her breath catch. Suddenly, she was again very aware of the fact that she was not a MacVie, that she was an English lady, and at the mercy of the black-eyed man whose gaze was unwavering.

The laughter trailed off and an awkward silence hung in the air as everyone else became aware of their unspoken exchange.

"'Tis time," Jack said.

Her nostrils flared. "Time for what?" she blurted. For a moment, she feared he had lied to her earlier about his intent to cause her no harm.

"For sleep," he said, standing.

She swallowed hard. "And where exactly will I be sleeping?"

He did not answer straightaway. He held her gaze and at length said, "Where ye'll be safest...with me."

Bella sucked in a sharp breath.

Rose jumped to her feet, hands on her hips and glared at Jack. "She most certainly will not sleep in yer hut. 'Tis indecent!"

Jack did not flinch. "I'm not concerned about decorum and decency. I'm responsible for everyone's safety including Lady Redesdale's. How do ye intend to keep her from escaping if she had a mind to do so?"

"Please," Bella began, her heart racing. "I will attempt nothing. You have my word."

Jack raised a brow at her. "A promise any captive would make. Ye're obviously not going to tell me if yer intentions were otherwise." Then he turned back to Rose. "I've not made this decision lightly."

Quinn stood up. "Rose, Jack is right. Our choices are few. We could bind her hands and feet, or, as Alec suggested, have her sleep in the hole."

Ian lunged to his feet, his eyes flashing with anger. "Quinn, I'll not hear mention of that again!"

Bella gasped at the sight of Ian's anger. In that moment, the youngest MacVie was a chilling sight, with his blue eyes set ablaze. How Quinn stood his ground, she would never know, but he did, holding out a steadying hand toward Ian as if he were a large, spooked animal. "I was not suggesting that we should, I was merely trying to demonstrate why having Lady Redesdale sleep in Jack's hut was the safest and gentlest of options."

"But I cannot sleep alone with a man," Isabella pleaded, feeling desperate—least of all a man whose kiss she knew to be both hard and tender all at the same time.

Jack cocked his brow at her. "If it's yer reputation that ye're fretting over, no one here has ever or will ever be invited to yer king's court."

Once again, she pledged not to attempt to leave their camp, but Jack would not be swayed. She looked beseechingly at the others.

"Sorry, lass," Rory said standing. Then he winked at her, and once more she was struck by his undeniable appeal. "Yer virtue is safer with Jack than with me." With his lips curved in a sensual grin, he turned and walked toward one of the huts.

Shifting her gaze, she looked at Ian who thus far had been her greatest champion. "Ye needn't fash yerself," the youngest brother assured her, his countenance once again, kind and gentle. "Jack is a man of honor."

Brows drawn she turned to Rose who could do naught but scowl at Jack before storming off in a huff.

Now, only she, Jack and Quinn remained. Isabella stared hard at Quinn who shifted in his seat for a moment before he stood and bowed. "I bid ye goodnight, Lady Redesdale."

It took all her restraint not to call after him and beg him not to leave her alone with Jack.

"'Tis time, Princess."

Her eyes locked with his. "Time for what?"

A smile tugged at one side of his lips. "I believe we've already established that 'tis time for sleep."

She arched a brow at him. "Sleep?"

"Ladies do sleep, do they not?" A glint of amusement shone in his eyes.

She lifted her chin and stood. "I see no humor in our situation." Tossing her hair over her shoulder, she strode past him in possession of her dignity—or so she had thought. Glancing back over her shoulder, she froze mid-step. He stared after her with that same quiet expression on his face that he had worn earlier. Her chest tightened as a smile tugged at the side of his lips.

Confused, she whirled back around and raced the rest of the way to his hut. Her heart pounded in her chest. She threw open the door, then slammed it behind her to vent her frustration, but the flimsy door was incapable of demonstrating her true state of upheaval.

Her gaze scanned the tiny room. Panic made her heart race even harder. At any moment, he would enter. She considered the small chest and lightweight table and chairs, but she knew that none of the sparse furnishings offered sufficient weight to keep Jack out.

The door opened.

Her breath hitched as he stepped into the small space, which seemed to shrink around her with the addition of his massive frame. She instinctively backed away, pressing against the thatched wall.

She was alone with a man who was both savior and captor. But at that moment, she certainly felt more captive than saved.

He stepped toward her, his gaze unreadable. Her heart pounded harder. "Ye must be tired," he said softly. His gaze held hers.

She stared up at him unable to speak. Her mind was suddenly fixated on the last time they had been alone in his hut. In that moment, her gaze traveled to his full lips, lips that had been pressed against her own.

She tried desperately to steer her thoughts toward the many reasons she should dislike the man standing in front of her, but as they continued to lock eyes, she felt as if she were drowning in a black sea.

He took a step toward her.

Her breath hitched.

Again, he stepped closer. His eyes bore into hers.

She fought to swallow, but her throat suddenly felt thick. He planted his hands on the wall on either side of her head. She opened her mouth to protest, but her objections remained lodged in her throat along with her thundering heart.

Surrounding her, he enclosed her in a cage of muscle and his all too familiar woody scent. He was so big and strong and smelled so good. He was unlike any man she had ever met. The intensity of his ebony gaze burned through her like wildfire.

He drew closer still.

She could hardly draw breath.

Slowly, he bent his head, lowering his lips until they were a breath away from hers. A sweet ache coiled in her stomach. She closed her eyes and waited, wanting to feel the sensual pressure of his lips, but it never came. A cool breeze caressed her cheek and forced open her eyes the instant before the door shut behind him.

Her knees gave way, and she slid to the ground, resting her head against the thatched wall. "Jack," she whispered.

Her mind was spinning out of control as the day's events combined with the tumult of new sensations coursing through her body. She gripped her stomach, feeling as though she would be sick again, but it was not bile that pushed for a way out. A wave of tears stung her eyes, and she collapsed beneath the weight of the day.

WITH HANDS IN TIGHT fists, Jack plowed his way through the grove. His heart thundered in his chest, igniting a searing pain that pulsed at his temples. He stormed around a copse of birch trees and passed into a small glen, heading straight for a clear, deep brook. Jerking his tunic over his head, he dove into the icy water and let the chill ease his body.

God above, he wanted her.

"Why?" he growled out loud.

He had spent less than a full day in her company, and here he was fixating on her, burning for her.

For pity's sake, he had nearly taken her against the wall.

And what drove him near to madness was that he was certain a part of her had welcomed his touch. He closed his eyes to better remember her parting lips and quick breaths as she held still, waiting for his kiss.

He should have taken her. What sort of lady would not fight the advances of a commoner, and a rebel thief at that? Perhaps she was free with her kisses and made light of her virtue with the English lords in her treacherous King's court. Were he a less honorable man, he might have claimed her for himself. Then, he would not now be paying for his self-control.

But he was not that sort of man.

With a curse, he dove once more beneath the surface of the pool. Water sluiced off his shoulders as he strode from the brook. His body remained hard and hungry for her, despite his cold bath. Pausing only to grab his tunic, he headed straight back through the woods no more relieved than before he set out. When his hut came into view, he stopped and forced his lungs to fill. Then, he blew out before taking another deep breath.

An English lady had no business occupying his thoughts. He had to remain focused on what mattered most—the many people dependent on him for their very survival. His attraction to Lady Redesdale was a physical and emotional betrayal on his part. How dare he dally with the enemy?

Striding past the pit fire, which had smoldered down to a pile of ash, he walked right up to his door and stopped. Lips pressed tightly, he considered his options. He never had any intention of forcing the lady to sleep with him in his hut. He had always planned to sleep just outside in front of the door, thus barring her way from escape. But if he were honest, sleeping with her was exactly what he wanted.

He reached for the door, but his fingers froze in midair. His already erect length grew harder just thinking about her stretched out beside him. His hand dropped. He lay down on the ground, lacing his fingers behind his head and stared up at the stars, trying to think of something other than silky brown hair and pale green eyes.

Scowling, he lifted his head off the ground.

Had he heard something?

He held his breath. A quiet, muffled noise reached his ears. It was she. He pressed his ear to the door. Mayhap, she slept but not soundly, and it was her unrest he heard.

A soft hiccup emanated from within.

Or perhaps she had the makings of a slight illness, and it was her blocked nose that he heard. Then an unmistakable whimper reached his ears, and he could no longer deny that she was crying.

"For pity's sake," he muttered, shaking his head. He stood up and eased the door open. There, in the middle of his pallet, she sat with her knees pulled tightly to her chest. Her shoulders shook as she sobbed into her hands, muffling the sound.

"Princess?" he said, quietly.

Her hands jerked away from her face, and she turned wide, glitteringly wet, exquisitely beautiful, pale green eyes on him.

His heart broke.

He had never been able to withstand a woman's tears. The hard front he had been struggling to hold in place since they had first met melted. At once, she was no longer Lady Redesdale. She was just Bella, a woman who had been through a great deal that day.

"Don't cry, Bella. Please don't cry."

Hugging her arms around her legs, she buried her face, hiding her tears.

"Go away," she sobbed.

He crossed to her and wrapped his arms around her. "Hush, lass," he crooned. Gently, he picked her up, cradling her in his arms. Her wet cheek pressed against his bare chest. He sat down on the chair and gently rocked her. Her soft body yielded to his.

"Never ye mind. Ye just cry it out, lass. Ye've earned yer tears."

Whether it was his urging or just the weight of the day, she did just that. Her arms came around his neck. He breathed in the lavender scent of her hair and held her tighter. Slowly, he stroked her back and whispered softly in her ear. "There, there, love. 'Twill be alright. Just let it out. Cry all ye want."

Her body trembled in his arms. Tears dripped down his chest. She buried closer to him, and he pressed a kiss to her brow. He let her cry until her tears ran dry. Then, even with her sorrow spent, she did not move but kept her arms around his neck. He savored their intimacy, and he continued to rock her, imagining the sea cradled them both.

After a while, the heat of her breath warmed his chest at regular intervals. He knew then that she had fallen asleep in his arms. Coming onto his knees, he laid her down. Gently, he tugged at her arm still wrapped around his neck, but she stirred. Having no desire to wake her, he stretched out beside her, pulling her into his arms.

Her head rested on his chest. His fingers grazed her silken skin. She nestled close.

"Damn," he muttered under his breath. "This feels good."

Chapter Eight

She stretched her arms above her head before rubbing the sleep from her eyes. The thatched roof came into focus and she jerked upright. The previous day's events came crashing down around her. She dug her hands into her unbound hair, remembering how the day had ended—with her sobbing in Jack's arms.

"Oh no," she groaned and fell back on the pallet. Perhaps, God would strike her dead right then and there and save her from the embarrassment of seeing Jack again. She held her breath and closed her eyes.

"You are meant to be a merciful God," she muttered, her gaze upturned.

She could hear activity outside. With a sigh, she stood, resigned now to her fate.

Standing, she smoothed the fabric of her borrowed tunic. In the light of day, she saw how tattered and stained the fabric was, but the secret to its softness was in the wear it had seen, which pleased her to no end. Digging around in Jack's trunk, she found a length of rope, which she used to belt her waist. Dressing for the day was usually an ordeal that required two maidservants. It was a wonder to her how quickly it could be done if one left off all the fuss as Jack had put it.

She worked the tangles free with her fingers, then swept her hair off her shoulders. She could not help the smile that curved her lips. Despite her questionable captivity, she had never felt so free.

Childish laughter outside her hut drew her attention. Stepping outside, she spied Rose sitting around the fire with five little girls.

Rose waved when she saw her. "Good morrow, Lady Redesdale."

Isabella hastened across the glade. "Good morrow, Rose."

"Well, ye seem well enough this morrow," Rose said, searching Isabella's face. "My brother behaved himself then?"

Bella blushed but nodded.

"I knew he would, but I still say he should have let ye bed down with me."

Wanting to change the subject, Isabella pointed to the basket in Rose's hand. "Where are you off to?"

"The lassies and I are going to break our fast by the stream. Would ye care to join us?"

"I would love to, but I'm not certain if I should." Bella scanned the camp, which appeared empty except for Rose and the girls.

Rose smiled. "The lads went hunting, but they'll be back soon. Do not fash yerself. Ye're safe with me."

"My role here is somewhat unclear. Am I allowed to go with you?"

"Well, ye must eat. Is that not true?"

As if to grant her permission, Bella's stomach growled loudly. Rose laughed. "Come on, pet. I've fresh bannock and dried meat."

Rose hooked arms with her, pulling her toward a narrow pass that cut through the trees. "I'd wager, they're as hungry as ye," Rose said, laughing as the girls darted ahead in a race.

"Who are they?" Isabella asked.

"Orphans," Rose replied.

Isabella raised a skeptical brow. "Orphans? Living in a camp among thieves?"

Rose smiled. "Things are not always as they seem, love."

Isabella nodded. That was one truth she had accepted long ago.

When they reached a stream, Rose pulled out two large blankets from her basket. Bella helped to spread the fabric under the shade of a large oak tree while two older girls unloaded the bread and meat. Bella guessed they both were near ten. When the food was spread about, one of the older girls took her by the hand.

"Sit," she said.

Bella knelt. Five little faces smiled at her. She smiled back and reached for a bannock. A faint whiff of steam rose from the firm cake. She held it to her nose and inhaled its warmth. "This is marvelous."

The girls giggled. The one who had taken her hand scooted closer. Bella admired her lovely dark braids and starry violet eyes. The girl took a bite of meat and while she chewed, she scrunched her eyes up at Bella. "Ye've lovely skin. 'Tis darker than mine."

Isabella smiled. "My olive skin was a gift from my mother. She was Sicilian."

The girl took another bite. "What's yer name?"

In her mind Bella recited her usual answer to that question—Lady Isabella Annunziatta Redesdale—but in the end her answer was simple: "Bella. And what is yours?"

"Moira. I'm Jack's lass."

Isabella's eyes widened in surprise. "I did not realize Jack had a daughter."

Moira laughed. "We are all Jack's lassies," she said, gesturing to the little girls littering the blankets.

Isabella's hand flew to her lips. "Oh my!" It was clear she needed to add womanizer to Jack's list of titles: Thief, commoner, Scotsman, and now rake.

Rose smiled and leaned close. "Do not fash yerself, my lady," she whispered.

"I'm hardly worried," Bella said as she straightened her skirt to avoid Rose's gaze. "Jack may father as many children as he likes."

Rose threw her head back with laughter. "I can tell ye on good authority that Jack has never fathered a child of his own." Rose's hand swept out to encompass the girls. "I told ye already. These girls are orphans, but they are in Jack's charge."

"I do not understand."

"Their parents were killed during the massacre. They were abandoned, left to die, in fact. Jack gathered them all and hid them. Abbot Matthew keeps this lot in the monastery. But there are many more than what ye see here. Jack has them spread throughout the countryside, some in homes with families, others in different monasteries, but he provides for every single one."

Once more Bella's eyes widened. "Do you mean to tell me this is what he does with his stolen gains? He feeds orphans."

"Aye," Rose said, still looking amused. "He robs English nobles and gives the money back to the Scottish people and to the cause, of course."

Bella leaned closer. "What cause?"

"Now, I like ye very much, but I won't be telling a Sassenach any more about that. No offense, my la—" Rose's words were cut off by a chorus of girlish squeals the instant before Jack's lassies took off back down the path.

"Jack," they cried.

Isabella's stomach flipped at the sight of him. He dropped to one knee and opened his arms. The girls threw themselves at him, knocking him onto his back. Isabella blushed at the sound of his rich laughter. Then she glimpsed red hair through the leaves as Ian came into view, followed by Rory, Quinn, and another man whom Isabella had not met, but given his height and black hair, she guessed he was the infamous Alec.

The sight of him made her stomach dance with nerves.

Ian cupped his hands around his mouth and shouted, "Wee lassies." Laughing, the girls scrambled to their feet and charged toward their new target.

Bella shifted her gaze back to Jack, who was still sprawled out on the ground. He lifted his head, and they locked eyes. His smile softened, but his gaze did not waver. And though she trembled and grew nervous, she also did not look away. His dark eyes bore into hers with a power to unlock yearning. She imagined night had found its source in their black depths. They blanketed her sensibility with coercive warmth.

He stood and walked toward her, his gaze ever constant. A shadow of a beard speckled his cheeks and strong jaw. Her heart pounded as he approached. She fought to swallow her nerves. He eased down onto the blanket. "Are ye feeling better today, Princess." His tone was void of yesterday's sarcasm.

She tore her eyes from his to hide her warm cheeks. "I am quite well, thank you," she said, still not daring to meet his gaze.

Then to her relief, one of the littlest girls scrambled onto Jack's lap.

He wrapped his arm around her. "Have ye met Florie?"

Bella reached out and tapped Florie's nose, earning a giggle in response. "I have. We were just breaking our fast together."

He rested his chin on the little girl's mop of blond curls. "I'm glad ye're feeling better."

Bella cleared her throat and straightened her back before she dared to meet his midnight eyes. He wore a plain linen tunic over simple brown hose. Black curls grazed his shoulders and fell across his eyes. He flashed a smile that forced her gaze to drop yet again. He was gorgeous, so raw and masculine and so very strong. She chewed her lip while she studied his hands. They were large and calloused. It was no wonder none of the men at court had been able to set her heart to race when there were men such as Jack in the world.

A breeze swept the glen, lifting her unbound hair from her shoulders. She closed her eyes and enjoyed the new sensation. Normally, if she were to venture outside, her hair and neck would have been confined by a fitted wimple. Only her face would have been exposed to the sun and wind. She laughed outright when the breeze quickened. "This is lovely," she said.

Jack nodded. "'Tis a beautiful stretch of earth."

"Indeed, it is," she said, quickly. "But I was speaking of the wind. You know what I am accustomed to wearing. Feeling the wind on my skin is a rare pleasure. It feels like freedom."

A sad smile curved his lips. "Freedom? I see little freedom surrounding us. We're all exiles, and ye're a lady bound by convention." He lifted Florie from his lap and turned her toward the other girls who were throwing rocks into the river with Ian. Then he stood and reached out a hand to help her up. "Freedom is an illusion—all anyone has are moments in time." He smiled and winked at her. "And more often than not, those moments must be stolen."

She smiled, feeling the power of his words. "Freedom is stolen moments." She took a deep breath, reveling in the ease of her clothing. "Look how quickly I've become a thief." Then she put her hand in his. He pulled her to her feet and stepped close.

"Would ye care to steal another moment?" he asked softly.

Her heart fluttered as she met his gaze. She nodded.

"Join me for a walk along the river, Princess?

Isabella looked down at her homespun dress. "I do not look the part of princess anymore."

His appreciative gaze traveled the length of her figure. "Nay," he breathed. "Ye do not."

"Call me Bella," she blushed and looked away embarrassed by her boldness.

He stepped closer still and crooked his thumb beneath her chin, forcing her gaze to meet his. "Shall we...Bella?" Her name he said in a whisper.

She nodded, not trusting herself to speak.

They walked for some time while Jack pointed out which herbs were best to flavor a stew and which had healing properties. She listened, savoring the sound of his deep voice. The sun slanted through the trees. Bird song filled the air, mingling with the distant laughter of Jack's family. Long had it been since she experienced such easy joy, and it filled her heart to the brim. They had walked in silence for some minutes when she looked at him sidelong. "I learned a little about you this morning."

He laughed. "Och, Rose is a good one for conversation."

"We may speak freely, may we not?"

"Aye, that we may."

"You are not truly a thief, are you?"

"I most certainly am. There are many who have stared down the length of my sword and handed over a bag of coin on fear of death."

She arched her brow at him. "I do not believe you would actually make good on your threat."

He winked at her and the simple gesture made her breath catch. "Ye're right," he said. "But they don't know that."

Now it was her turn to laugh. "If your victims could see you surrounded by little girls, they would, no doubt, fume over being duped into believing you were a villain."

"What do ye think of my lassies?" he asked.

"They are lovely girls."

"They are kept hidden in the monastery while I continue to find them homes." A shadow of worry passed over his features. "It has been five years. Many of these girls came to me as babies. I fear they will spend the remainder of their youth with the abbot and will likely go to a convent when they are old enough."

She stopped then and turned to look at the water rushing past. "It really has been five years, hasn't it?" she said absently.

"It has," he said.

Her chest tightened around the familiar pain. "It feels as though it has been only five minutes."

He grabbed her arm and turned her about. Brows drawn together in a frown, he said, "Ye were there? Ye were in Berwick during the Massacre?"

Confused by his sudden harshness, she tried to yank her arm free, but his grip tightened. She winced. "I was. Now release me!"

He looked down at his hand squeezing her arm. His eyes widened, and he let go. He stepped back and raked his hand through his hair. "I thought ye'd come to Berwick after Edward had claimed the city for England."

She shook her head. "I was born there. My mother and father met among the market stalls." She turned away and cast her gaze towards the trees alongside the stream. Their small spring leaves shone in the sun, and she wondered how such destructive hate could exist amid such wondrous beauty.

"I loved Berwick." Her voice broke. "It was a great city." Tears stung her eyes. "No!" she said, scolding herself. Fighting to ignore her aching heart, she stormed away, but he caught her arm and once more swung her around. Her hands covered her face. "I don't want to cry anymore."

JACK HAD GLIMPSED THE barren ache in her eyes the instant before she hid her pain behind her hands. His own eyes squeezed shut against the reminder of loss. When his mind had quieted, he once again looked at Bella, but it was as if for the first time. He no longer saw the spoiled daughter of a lord. He saw her desperation and the yearning echoed by his own heart. It was a struggle to move beyond the rubble and blood, to find a life worth living again. He reached out and grazed his fingertips down her hands still covering her face. Then he gently pulled her into his arms. "Who did ye lose, Bella?"

Her hands fell away. She pressed her lips together and swiped at her wet eyes, but she still did not meet his gaze. "My mother," she whispered. And then her eyes locked with his. "And my father."

"They were both slain in the chaos?"

She shook her head. "My mother was stabbed through the heart and her head split open." A sob tore from her throat, and she covered her mouth with her hands. "My father survived those days, untouched by blade or fire. His body lives, but he does not reside inside of it. Every day I lose a little more of him to his grief. He shuts out life and me along with it." She sagged in his arms. "Five years have passed, but it has not truly ended. The world is still on fire."

He lifted her into his arms and carried her further down the bank of the stream to a slope, shaded beneath a large oak tree. He sat, cradling her in his arms and rocked her gently. Then he pulled away just enough to see her face.

"Our youngest sister, Roslyn set out that morning to help my mother sell apples." His voice cracked. "My parents were also slain." Expelling a long, slow breath, he rested his head back against the tree and stroked her soft waves. The song of the stream surrounded them. He swallowed the remainder of his lament and waited for the familiar numbness to return. After a time, she sat up and dabbed at her eyes with the edge of her tunic. Still holding her in his lap, he grazed his hand down her thigh, touching the tattered fabric. "Forgive me for giving ye such an ugly tunic to wear."

She shrugged. "If it is so ugly, then you won't mind if I never give it back."

"Could an English lady used to silk and lace truly be happy in homespun wool?"

She smiled and breathed out a heavy breath. He could see the tension ease from her shoulders. "I already am."

His gaze passed over her olive skin as he studied her face. "We aren't so different," he breathed.

Pale green eyes locked with his. "It would seem not."

For a moment, he almost believed he had found himself in her heart, but then truth raised its ugly head. Suddenly, he was staring across an endless, uncrossable gray chasm, to where she stood, draped in wondrous colors that his rough hands could never hold. His heart sank as he forced the truth from his lips. "Except that ye're a noblewoman and I, a commoner."

To his surprise, she reached out and cupped his cheek. "I am the daughter of Lord David Redesdale but also of Annunziatta Santospirito." Tears once more filled her eyes, but she smiled through them. "And she was the daughter of an Italian merchant. She was a commoner, but there was nothing common about her. And I see nothing common about you, Jack MacVie."

A rush of fire exploded in his heart. He cupped her face between his hands and lightly pressed his lips to hers. She trembled. Then her arms came around his neck. He dug his fingers into her thick hair, and she leaned into him. Their lips and tongues moved in unison as the world faded away. Chest heaving, she tore her lips free. "I do not understand what is happening!"

He pressed his forehead to hers. "Neither do I," he said, breathlessly.

"Jack," a deep voice shouted, intruding upon the moment.

He jerked around. Quinn raced toward them.

"'Tis Bishop Lamberton. He just arrived and wishes to speak to ye and the lady."

Jack's chest tightened. He looked down at her. Slowly, he pulled her arm from around his neck and brought her palm to his lips. Then, he dropped her hand and stepped back, putting space between them. "Our stolen moment is over, Lady Redesdale."

Chapter Nine

Jack had first met Bishop Lamberton on the open road shortly after the massacre. He, Quinn, and Alec had set out to hunt one morning, leaving behind Rose, Rory, and Ian to tend to dozens of newly orphaned children they had hidden in the woods.

After all, empty bellies needed to be filled.

When they spied the bishop's carriage approaching, Jack and his brothers hid their bows and full quivers in the brush to conceal that they'd been hunting on monastic land. But the bishop had been kind and bade them not be afraid. Before too long, he was able to pull the truth from Jack. Believing the Bishop's concern for Scotland's children to be genuine, Jack led the holy man through the woods to their hastily made camp. The Bishop held true to his word that he would help the orphans. He opened his arms to the children, comforting them with kind words and prayers.

Later that day, the Bishop took Jack to meet with the abbot at the monastery. Abbot Matthew not only gave permission to Jack and his band of youthful exiles to remain on monastic lands, but he also gave them food and supplies.

It did not take Jack long to realize he had made two powerful allies.

The Bishop visited regularly. On one occasion he had arrived when the MacVie brothers were practicing swordplay with sticks, their favorite pastime since they were lads. To Jack's surprise, the bishop left after only a brief stay, but he returned later that day with swords for each of them.

Taking Jack aside, the bishop put his arm around him and said, "You have the skill, my son, which the good Lord has given you." Then he took Jack's hand and solemnly wrapped his fingers around the hilt of his new sword. "Now, you have the tools, which *I* have given you."

Less than a week later, the bishop came again, only this time he brought five black masks and five shirts of gleaming black mail.

And so, the Saints were born.

With the support of Bishop Lamberton and Abbot Matthew, Jack and his brothers became highwaymen for a higher cause. By robbing the English nobility riding north into Scotland, Jack provided for the children in his charge and contributed toward the bishop's first concern—fighting for Scottish independence.

Long had it been since Jack first pulled on his black-hooded mask. Over the years, he had always looked forward to a visit from the bishop. But this time, his heart felt heavy, for he knew the bishop had come to address the matter of the English lady in their company.

As Jack approached the holy man with Bella on his arm, the older man made the sign of the cross and blessed them both. Then he turned his attention to Bella. "Are you well, my lady?"

Bella dipped in a low curtsy. "I am, Your Excellency."

The old man flashed Jack a brief smile. "And I trust, my friends have shown you every due respect."

But Jack cringed inwardly when he remembered Alec's suggestion to throw Bella into the hole, not to mention Jack's stolen kisses. He closed his eyes waiting for Bella to confess all to the good bishop, but she merely smiled. "They have all behaved like perfect gentlemen."

Jack looked down at her. Her eyes locked with his and did not waver.

Bishop Lamberton cleared his throat, snaking Jack's attention. "We have a situation. You were right not to leave the lady defenseless in the wood, but she cannot remain here even a moment longer."

Jack pressed his lips together. He wished it otherwise, but he knew the bishop was right. An English lady gone missing in Scotland meant trouble for everyone. "What is yer plan?"

"We must return her to her father," the bishop stated.

Jack nodded. "I will take her."

"You, an exile and rebel? That is a truly dreadful idea. The only thing worse would be to include your brothers in your folly. Then, you can all be captured and hung together. Aye, I'm sure Rose will be thrilled by your idea." The bishop shifted his gaze to Bella. "Abbot Matthew will take ye. He will tell your father that you were found by men of his order in the wood and that you were safeguarded within the monastery, which, by the by, is where you will sleep tonight," he said, shifting his gaze to look pointedly at Jack. Then his attention returned to Bella. "The less the good abbot has to lie, the better." A smile crinkled the bishop's kind eyes. "Although, to combat the tyranny of men, even the godliest must bend the rules," he said with a wink. Then he offered her his arm. "Come, Lady Redesdale. I shall take you to the monastery myself. You leave tomorrow at first light."

The Bishop had a firm grasp on Bella's arm as he walked toward his carriage. Panic seized her. She jerked away.

"Is there something the matter, my child?" the bishop asked, turning back to look at her with questioning eyes.

Her mind raced. She had no answer for the bishop. Certainly, she knew she should be relieved. She wanted to go home—did she not? Then she met Jack's dark eyes and knew he was the reason her feet refused to move.

He was like no man she had ever met. She thought of the children he had saved and how much he had suffered. He was still a thief, a commoner, and a Scotsman, but he was also a hero.

Her hero.

"Lady Redesdale," the Bishop said.

She tore her eyes from Jack's and looked at the bishop. "We must away," he urged. "No good can come of you staying here a moment longer. No good for anyone," he said with a pointed look at Jack.

She nodded and bit her lip to fight back the tears that suddenly filled her eyes. That was it then. She was to say goodbye and never see Jack again. She would return to Berwick, trapped within the walls of her home where she would wait for her wedding to Hugh. She was Lady Redesdale after all, and English ladies did not marry thieving Scotsman—no matter how compelling or forbidden.

"Lady Redesdale," the bishop said with stern urgency.

She jerked her eyes once more away from Jack's. "Forgive me, Your Excellency," she whispered. Then she turned back to

Jack and dipped into a low curtsy. "Thank you," she said before she turned and followed the bishop.

Bishop Lamberton climbed inside his carriage and offered her his hand. She reached out, but then her breath hitched as someone grabbed her from behind. She jerked around and saw a flash of Jack's black eyes the instant before his lips claimed hers and the world fell away. Her soul cried out, knowing it had found its mate. His lips molded to hers. His scent engulfed her. She longed never for the moment to end. Wrapping her arms around his neck, she gave herself over to him. In that moment, she knew that the angels had put her in Jack's path.

But they were not in heaven where angels reigned.

Men made rules that controlled her life.

Jack tore his lips away. His breath coming in great heaves.

"That will have to be enough," the bishop said behind her, not unkindly.

It could never be enough.

Jack stepped away, his black eyes burning through her soul. She sat beside the bishop, all the while never breaking eye contact with Jack. She watched him as the carriage pulled ahead. She traced every line of his broad shoulders and strong features into memory.

"Drink your fill, my lady," the bishop said softly at her side. "For you will never see him again."

Chapter Ten

Isabella followed behind a tall, lanky monk with a stooped back. Despite his gangly appearance, he walked like a swiftly moving cloud, soundlessly gliding down the narrow halls of Haddington Monastery. They passed through a maze of shadowy corridors lit by torches. She felt as though they were burrowing into the dark belly of a mountain. The silent monk turned down yet another hallway. Along each side were roughhewn wooden doors. At the end of the hallway, he opened a door, revealing a small but clean cell. The furnishings consisted of a narrow wooden platform, which had a folded blanket on top of it, and a small table with a candle and wooden rosary beads.

Bishop Lamberton had warned her to expect modest accommodations. She was not bothered by the poverty of her surroundings, but the gloom was hard to bear. With a heavy sigh, she spread out the blanket upon the hard planks and laid down. The candle flickered, casting dancing shadows upon the low ceiling. Her gaze moved across the surface, becoming a bare canvas for her to paint her dreams. In her mind's eye, she easily conjured Jack's image as though he were hovering above her, just out of reach.

The imaginary Jack looked at her with sensual yearning. Still, he raised a scolding eyebrow at her. *Ye know I shouldn't be here, Princess.*

"I know, but who could find out," she said aloud. "There is no one here but us."

Princess, ye're alone. I'm only a fantasy.

"I know that, but now I do not feel so lonely. So why don't you just cooperate and call me Bella?"

As ye wish, Bella.

She smiled and blushed despite knowing she talked only to herself and not to him.

"I love how you kiss me," she said softly, confessing what she wished she could to the real Jack. "It is so different from Hugh's kisses."

Her imaginary Jack scowled. *Who's Hugh?*

She shrugged her shoulders. "He was my best friend in my youth. Now, he's my betrothed."

Were ye not going to tell me ye're to be married? her pretend Jack growled.

"There was hardly time between you rescuing me, offending me, and then sweeping me off my feet."

Don't change the subject, Princess. Who is he? A stuffy English lord with pasty skin and soft hands.

She nodded. "He is soft compared to you, but he is also a good man."

If he is so wonderful, why am I here, and not Sir Hugh?

"He is a lord actually."

Jack's scowl deepened. *Fine. Why am I here, and not Lord La di da?*

A sad smile curved her lips at her imagined jest. "He doesn't stir my soul," she whispered.

Jack flashed his sideways grin. *And I do?*

"Yes." Her hands flew to cover her face. Then she took a deep breath and dropped her hands. He smiled at her, his eyes full of feeling.

I wish ye could be mine, Bella.

Brows drawn, she shook her head. "Surely, there is a way."

His smile diminished, and his eyes grew dark with yearning.

Nay, lass. I am a Scotsman, and ye're my enemy.

Her heart sank as his image faded. Blinking back tears, she stared at the cold, hard ceiling. If she could not make a romance with Jack work even in her dreams, then surely it was hopeless.

More than ever, she wished she had never set out to visit her sister. Before, she had felt listless and wanting, but she had no taste of desire and no face to imagine. Now, she would have to walk through life trapped by a wimple and a passionless marriage, all the while knowing the feel of strong hands on her skin.

She turned on her side, curled into a ball, closed her eyes, and again and again, she relived her last kiss with Jack.

Chapter Eleven

A soft rapping on the door stirred Isabella awake. She winced, feeling a dull ache throb at her temples. Staring up at the ceiling overhead, she willed Jack's image to appear. But her despair was too great. The weight of her heavy heart pinned her to the hard platform bed. She drew a shallow breath and closed her eyes, wishing to retreat into slumber, but the knocking grew louder. Whoever waited outside her cell was not going to leave her to her misery.

Wiping sleep from her eyes, she stood and pulled open the door. The tall, stooped monk who had been her guide the night before stood with eyes downcast. Once again, he did not speak but motioned for her to follow. Once again, they wound through narrow hallways, back the way they'd come.

The crisp morning air helped to revitalize her senses as she stepped out into the small courtyard. Shadow still hung heavy in the sky. She filled her lungs with fresh air, glad to be free from the confines of the cloisters, but her relief was short-lived. Expelling the breath with distaste, she realized that it was a treacherous lie, as potent as any betrayal. Within the tantalizing, crisp morning air one breathed the day's beginnings—its very origins. But her day, like all her days, was stagnant before she'd even taken her first breath.

It was the same for countless women who had come before her—women with voices unheard. Women with passions left to wane until all desire faded. The space afforded her life was a fraction of the size of the monks' starved cells. She was crammed into a dark hole, and the world ignored her screams. Her fists clenched. She would relinquish every luxury of the body to feel the richness of soul that only love could provide. She would rejoice in the feel of rough wool on her skin if the hands that swept her tunic from her body stoked her passion.

"My lady?"

Her head jerked up and she met Abbot Matthew's kind, patient eyes. She cleared her throat and uncurled her fingers.

"The wagon is ready." He gestured toward the open gate. Monks with hoods pulled low over their faces as if in prayer waited for her to join them on the benches lining the sides of a rough-hewn wagon. Their solemn reception mirrored her life—disciplined and stark, void of the pleasures that ignite the spirit.

Freedom is stolen moments.

Jack's words hit her hard in the gut. She was no thief. If freedom was stolen, she was doomed to be chained.

She had tasted rapture. Her blood had ignited. Her soul struck deep with a yearning, but now it was left cold and hollow. How could she return to the echoing grandness of her lonely fortress? She pictured the vast, empty rooms full of lost dreams and teeming sorrows. Very soon, she would leave behind one prison to join Hugh in another—his fortress in the heart of Berwick.

The despair in her heart swelled when her thoughts turned to her once beloved city. The English king's defensive walls would be higher than when she'd left. In that moment, they became waves in her mind, high and fierce, crashing around her, swallowing her youthful heart.

But she was not meant to be caged!

With word and deed her parents had taught her that love was as essential to life as water or food. It sustained one's soul.

Her tall, gangly monk bowed to her before taking her elbow and helping her climb into the wagon. None of the monks already seated moved from their pious positions while she claimed her place on one of the benches.

Before too long, the wagon pulled forward, led by a team of donkeys. They passed through the gates. She glimpsed the sun peeking out from beneath the horizon. Tears stung her eyes as she gave her despair over to the soft pink light. It tinted the morning fog, which writhed and shifted across the surface of a distant lake, but its sensual dance made her long to feel Jack's lips on her skin. She closed her eyes against the dawn and allowed the countryside to pass unseen. Their journey could never be long enough. Too soon she would be home where the towering city walls would block her view north into Scotland...where love dwelled.

Pounding hooves caused her eyes to open. She stood. A dozen knights approached on horseback, carrying banners bearing the Trevelyan coat of arms. Her heart sank when she spied Hugh riding in the lead.

"Bella!"

He had seen her. Her heart pounded in her ears. She took a deep breath and prayed for strength. She could not deny her truth. Despite how she might wish otherwise, she was Lady Isabella Redesdale. Sweeping her unbound hair away from her face, she knotted it demurely at the nape of her neck.

"Abbot Matthew," she said, her voice steady, though beneath the surface of her calm I, she struggled against the inevitable. "Stop, please. The lord approaching is my betrothed."

"Yer what?" She heard a voice say.

She sat down and stared at the monk in front of her. His body was still, his head solemnly bowed. Her gaze followed the outline of broad shoulders.

Could it be he?

She clasped her hands in her lap to conceal how her fingers shook and leaned forward in her seat. Narrowing her eyes, she strained to see through his ink black hood.

"Isabella!" Hugh's voice jarred her from her trance.

"I am here," she called, though her gaze remained fixed on the monk.

"Praise be to Mary and all the Saints, you're alive." The wagon shook as Hugh climbed onto the back.

She had no choice but to look at her betrothed. He stood with open arms. Forcing a smile to her lips, she rose but shifted her gaze back to the monk in front of her. Once more her gaze traced his broad shoulders.

It was Jack. She was certain.

His closeness stole her breath. All she had to do was reach out and she could once more wrap her arms around his neck.

Throw back your hood, her thoughts commanded. *Claim me as yours.*

Still, the monk did not break his solemnity.

Hugh crossed to her side. "Are you hurt? Can you not walk?"

Mayhap her heart played with her mind. Mayhap the man across from her was a monk and in desperation she imagined Jack's voice. She swallowed her hope and turned to face Hugh.

His fine, blue eyes held nothing but tenderness and concern. She tried to speak, but the words stuck in her dry throat.

"My flask," Hugh said to his footman who hastened to carry out his bidding.

She closed her eyes and allowed him to tip the flask to her lips. The rush of liquid brought her throat back to life. At last, she found the will to answer his question. "I am well, my lord."

He smiled with relief. "You cannot imagine my fear. Word of the attack arrived just after midnight." He stroked his fingers down her cheek. "I thought I would never see you again." She dropped her eyes in shame. Hugh was all things decent and good, her dearest friend from youth. Why could she find no love for him in her heart?

"Come, my darling," he said, wrapping his arm around her shoulders. "I will take you home."

She nodded, allowing him to draw her forward. As she stepped past the monk, she let her handkerchief drop from her fingertips at his feet. Gaze downcast, she watched strong fingers dart out from long, black sleeves to seize it.

Jack.

Her chest tightened. She could not breathe. Her legs trembled, ready to give way. Hugh's arm came under her knees and lifted her, holding her close. He pressed a kiss to her brow. "I am here now," he whispered. "You need not fear, not anymore." He passed one of his guards. She listened numbly to his command. "Take four men and ride with the monks to Berwick. Lord Redesdale and I will hear their testimony. The rest of you ride with me." He set her on the saddle, then swung up behind her. His horse leapt forward as they galloped away.

Hugh held her close. "I know your heart as well as my own, Bella. I will take you away from here and back to Berwick as fast as my horse will ride."

Fresh tears filled her eyes. Regarding the contents of her heart, Hugh could not have been more wrong.

JACK REMAINED STILL, his head bowed as if in solemn prayer, despite how he yearned to cast aside the monk's cloak and chase after Bella and her betrothed. His chest tightened. That fiend of a lord had called her Bella.

But she was his Bella.

His fingers curled into tight fists, but she wasn't—not really. Apparently, she belonged to another man.

Silently, he cursed his lack of foresight. Of course she was betrothed. After all, she was a lady with title and duty.

What had he been thinking?

Well, that was just it—he hadn't been thinking, only feeling, yearning for a woman who had no business even talking to the likes of him. Despite her mother's humble birth, she was still an English noble.

He glanced down at the handkerchief in his hand and stroked his thumb over the "B" elaborately embroidered with silver thread.

"So, Saint Peter is now Brother Peter."

Jack's shoulders stiffened. It was Abbot Matthew who spoke. He lifted his head and cast off the black hood. Cool, spring air swept over his neck and ears, exposed now by his newly shorn hair.

"Good morrow, Abbot."

The older man gestured to the seat beside him. Jack stood and climbed onto the driver's seat. The abbot snapped the reins, and they set off toward Berwick with the English guards in lead.

"How long have ye known it was me?" Jack said.

The abbot smiled. "I know every member of my order at a glance, even with their hoods drawn."

Jack dipped his head to show that he knew he had underestimated his old friend.

"Anyway, ye're twice the size of any monk I've ever known," the abbot said, chuckling. "So, which of yer brothers is back there?"

A smile tugged at Jack's lips. "Quinn."

"I suspected as much," the abbot said. "Saint Augustine is now Brother Augustine." He shook his head. "Ye ken Bishop Lamberton will not like this."

Jack shrugged. "It could not be helped."

"Then ye've decided to fight for her?"

Jack looked the abbot hard in the eye. "I'm not leaving Berwick without her, even if I have to abduct her again." His gaze shifted. He looked at the road ahead and then at the tired team of donkey's easing them forward at a snail's pace. "Could we go any faster?"

The abbot pulled a little on the reins, slowing their progress. "The wait is yer penance for lying to me and stowing away on my wagon."

Jack seized the reins from the abbot's hands and snapped them hard against the donkeys' backs. "I'll go to confession." They surged forward. "Forgive me, old friend, but I've a prize to steal."

Chapter Twelve

Jack's gaze swept over the comforts of the Redesdale solar. A massive hearth filled one side of the room. Colorful tapestries covered the walls. Elaborately carved, high-backed chairs, like the one he sat in, dominated the room's center. Doubt gripped his heart. He would never be able to give Bella such comfort, not in ten lifetimes. Exhaling a quiet breath, he bowed his head and forced himself to relax. In front of him sat Lord Hugh Trevelyan, Isabella's betrothed, and to his left, Lord Redesdale. Isabella's father had glanced their way when Jack, Quinn, and Abbot Matthew had first entered his solar, but that was his only acknowledgment of their presence. His gaze remained fixed on the low burning fire. Given Lord Redesdale's apparent apathy, Jack was not surprised when it was Lord Trevelyan who first addressed the abbot.

"Lady Redesdale's carriage was discovered by Lord Widdrington who was marching to Dunbar. His messenger rode first to Berwick Castle where King Edward sits in residence. At once, the king ordered dozens of guards north to recover my lady and to find the beasts who butchered her guard; however, Lord Redesdale and I did not receive word of the attack until the earliest hours of this very day. As far as I know, none of the villains have been caught." Lord Trevelyan leaned forward in his seat and stared hard at the abbot. "That is all we know. Now, it is your turn. How came you to find Lady Redesdale?"

The abbot straightened in his seat. "Brothers from my order witnessed the attack." He gestured to Jack. "Brother Peter was included in their number."

Jack raised his gaze from the floor and locked eyes with Lord Trevelyan. Jack was a good judge of character, and as much as he wanted to despise the English lord, Jack could not deny his display of honor. Lord Trevelyan had treated the Scottish monks with every due respect. He was attentive to Lord Redesdale. He had even shown kindness to the servants who had arrived moments after they had entered with trenchers of food and ale.

Jack glanced at Quinn. He could not tell Lord Trevelyan the truth of Bella's rescue. After all, they were supposed to be monks, not warriors able to charge on horseback through bands of criminals.

Jack cleared his throat. "We heard the attack from further down the road—"

"Why were you so far from your monastery?" Lord Trevelyan interrupted.

Jack fought the sudden urge to shift in his chair. He was not familiar with the customs of monastic life.

Abbot Matthew spoke before Jack could. "The road cuts through the outskirts of monastic lands, my lord. My fellow brothers were still within our boundaries."

Lord Hugh nodded and gestured for Jack to continue. "When we heard the clash of blades, we circled back and hid among the trees, observing the struggle. The lady was pulled from her carriage, but she managed to escape into the woods. We rushed to her aid and retreated deep into the forest. They never found our trail." The image of Bella's near rape flooded his mind, but he forced the memories away. Neither her father nor her betrothed needed to know the great danger Bella had been in. "We returned to the monastery with Lady Redesdale. She was blessed to be free from harm. After she had rested, we set out to bring her home."

Lord Trevelyan nodded. "She did not suffer injury, although she is subdued, I'm certain from the shock of the ordeal." He frowned. "But I am afraid greater harm has been done. Rumors abound, claiming the attack was not the act of common thieves, but rebellious Scottish peasants. I fear this incident will be used to renew border violence."

Jack pressed his lips together in a frown and thought back to the attack. "Their number surpassed twenty men, my lord. I must agree that this was no common raid."

Lord Trevelyan shrugged. "But twenty is not so great a number if they were exiles. I've heard of such camps existing, outcasts and outlaws who've come together."

Jack nodded. "Hidden within the northern forests are small villages of people as ye've described. Still, they would not tinker in so large a number, at least not in the light of day."

Lord Trevelyan expelled a long breath. "Then the rumors are true. Damn," Jack heard him mutter. "Our borders have been peaceful for some weeks. I for one welcomed the respite from war."

Jack moved to the edge of his seat. "I said it was no simple raid, but I can also tell ye they weren't Scottish peasants."

Brows drawn, Lord Trevelyan leaned back in his seat. "Are you suggesting, they were English peasants?"

Jack shook his head. "Whether Scottish or English, I cannot say. But I've one certainty—they weren't peasants."

"How can you be so sure?"

Surprised, Jack turned to look at Lord Redesdale who had been the one to pose the question.

"The men who attacked your daughter's carriage showed every physical sign of excellent health. They were men used to an abundant table. And the skill with which they fought belied their meager dress."

Lord Redesdale did not reply. Once more, he shifted his gaze away from Jack to stare at the flames. A sadness stole into Jack's thoughts. He remembered Bella telling him that following her mother's death, her father had shut life out and her along with it. It was clear to Jack that Lord Redesdale had retreated into himself.

But why?

Jack knew the hardship of grief, but grief alone could not have taken Lord Redesdale from the world. Only shame held that power. But what shame did Bella's father carry?

A knock at the door stole Jack's attention.

A young maidservant opened the door after Lord Trevelyan gave command. She announced that the hour for supper had arrived.

JACK HAD NEVER BEEN inside one of the large fortresses within Berwick. When he had resided in the city, he had lived in a one room, wooden home, shared with his parents and six siblings. Until now, he had never known that one could be inside and yet feel so entirely unconfined. The ceilings might have grazed the heavens they were so tall. Flickering candlelight resembled stars studding the night sky. After his captain's ship would make port, he had often slept on board beneath the stars rather than returning to their cramped home. He closed his eyes and for a moment he was out there, once more on the sea, moving to the rhythm of the waves.

His eyes flew open and followed ribbons of smoke coiling up from the central hearth, then out a vent in the roof. Already Bella had the sky—what could he give her?

He fought to chase the self-doubt from his thoughts, but his heart felt heavy as his gaze shifted to the mantle place above the hearth, which bore a large shield with the Redesdale coat of arms. For a moment, he felt as though the grandness were closing in around him. He had no title to give Bella. He could not even offer her an honest name—Jack MacVie was a thief. He reached into the sleeve of his monk's habit and felt her soft handkerchief.

Quinn nudged him. "'Tis like a tomb in here."

Jack raised a skeptical brow. "Ye've lofty aspirations for yer final resting place."

"Look around ye," Quinn whispered.

Jack's shoulders tensed. "Trust me. I have."

"'Tis barren and cold."

At first, Jack did not know what Quinn meant, but then he considered the empty tables and strange, almost eerie, silence. At the high dais sat only Lord Redesdale who had not looked up from his plate since first taking his seat. Despite the warm fire and bright tapestries, the room was as Quinn had described, cold. Once again, Jack's gaze swept over his surroundings, and he realized that an oppressive gloom hung in the air, pushing out life and laughter.

"'Tis no wonder she came looking for ye," Quinn said whispered.

Jack cocked a brow at his brother. "She was attacked, her virtue nearly stolen, and then we abducted her. She did not set out looking for me."

Quinn smiled. "Aye, but she did find ye, and thank God above for that. She'll suffocate in here."

The arched doorway opened, stealing Jack's attention. A manservant came into the room. "Lord Trevelyan and Lady Redesdale," he announced, his voice echoing off the tall ceiling.

Jack tensed. This would be the first time he would look upon her since arriving in Berwick. Sweat beaded his brow. Their bench scraped the floor as he, Quinn, the abbot, and the other monks stood out of respect for the lady of the house. Jack pressed his lips tight to silence the snarl that fought to be released as Isabella appeared in the doorway on Lord Trevelyan's arm.

Her olive skin stood out in sharp contrast against the white of her fitted wimple. Sweeping down from her elaborate headdress were layers of silken veils. He sought her gaze as she passed by, but her eyes remained downcast. His gaze followed her across the length of the great hall and then to the high dais where she sat next to her betrothed. At once, servants brought them ale and one trencher of food to share.

He stared at her, willing her to look his way, but she kept her gaze aloft. She looked out the windows, at the hearth, anywhere but at him. He clenched his teeth while Lord Trevelyan leaned close to whisper something in her ear. She smiled at first and then laughed outright. Her gaze held warmth when she looked at her betrothed; he could see her affection for him even from across the room. Lord Trevelyan looked up then and locked eyes with Jack. A friendly smile played at the lord's lips. He stood and raised his cup high. "I drink to the health of the good Benedictine Brothers. Thank you for your aid in restoring Lady Redesdale back to her family." Hugh took a long sip from his cup, then placed a hand on Bella's shoulder. "Have you kind words you wish to bestow upon our humble yet heroic company?"

Jack held his breath and waited for her to turn his way. His heart hammered in his ears while she kept her silence. At last, she looked up and they locked eyes, for a moment, a breath, but then she turned back to her betrothed. "I have nothing to say."

Jack's nostrils flared. Her rejection cut deep.

"Brother Peter," the abbot said quietly, leaning past Quinn to look at Jack. "Yer face has gone from red to purple. Remember the robe ye wear. A monk does not look with daggers at his host."

Jack shifted his gaze to his food and took a deep breath. 'Did ye eat my pigeon pie?" he whispered accusingly to Quinn.

"Wheest, Jack," Quinn whispered. "Get a hold of yerself. Pigeon pie was three courses ago."

Jack leaned back while a servant removed his untouched plate and set yet another course in front of him. The waste provoked his ire to new heights. He pushed the bench back and stood. It was either leave that very moment or reveal the truth of his identity by behaving in the most unholy manner. Another second within the hall while she dangled her lord and her wealth in front of him and he was going to storm the high dais and beat Lord Trevelyan to within an inch of life.

"Brother Peter," Quinn hissed, but Jack ignored him and convention all together. He rose and stormed around the table and straight out the door. He had come for Bella, but she was nowhere to be found. In her stead was the Lady Redesdale, cold and confined, and of no interest to him.

Chapter Thirteen

Bella fought to conceal her panic as she watched Jack storm from the great hall. "Brother Peter must be ill," she said to Hugh, maintaining a casual tone. Hugh stood and offered her his hand. "See that his needs are met, but do not stay away long." He kissed her hand.

She dipped in a low courtesy and walked calmly from the high dais, despite how she longed to race after Jack, which is just what she did the instant after the door to the great hall shut behind her. She tore down the hallway and out into the courtyard. Scanning the shadows, she strained to glimpse his silhouette in the darkness.

"Brother Peter," she shouted when she saw him pass under torchlight near the stable doors.

He stopped but did not turn around. She rushed to his side, clasping his strong arm. "You must allow me to explain myself."

He did not look at her. "Ye've already said enough," he said, his voice laced with bitterness.

She pulled him into the stables. Torchlight from the courtyard cast a dim glow inside. She could just make out the stony set to his lips and the hard glint in his dark eyes. She swallowed the knot in her throat. "But I have said nothing. I could not speak to you, not in front of Hugh and my father."

"Of course ye couldn't. How could the great Lady Redesdale condescend to address a commoner?"

She grabbed the front of his robe and pressed herself against him. "I dared not speak to you in front of them," she hissed. She held her breath, her heart aching in her chest. She stared up into his midnight eyes. "I was afraid they would guess my feelings for you."

His shoulders and face softened. "Bella," he whispered, wrapping his arms around her.

She leaned into him. Her body flooded with warmth.

"Bella," he said louder, his voice hoarse. He seized her in a crushing embrace, his gaze boring into hers. "Say it, Bella. Say what ye feel."

Her heart quaked. Breathless, she wrapped her arms around his neck and closed her eyes. "I've fallen in love with you, Jack."

Her breath hitched when his lips claimed hers. She melted into his strong arms, his scent surrounding her. Desire burned through her veins, but her conscience fought against the flame. She pushed him away, shaking her head. "Please, help me, because I cannot."

He reached for her, drawing her back into his arms. "Ye can't marry him," he whispered, pressing his forehead to hers.

A chill passed through her. "But I do not wish to hurt him. He is my friend and a good man."

"Too good," he growled, jerking away. The stony set to his face returned, causing her chest to tighten, but then he expelled a long breath. She watched his shoulders loosen. Slowly, he stepped back and leaned against the stable wall, closing his eyes. She ached to touch him, but her feet remained fixed to the floor. He continued to keep his gaze from hers. Her breathing quickened. She fought to swallow the painful lump that had gathered in her throat.

His eyes slowly started to open. He looked at her though half-closed lids. "I never dreamed of a woman like ye. I wouldn't have dared." Her stomach fluttered at the sight of his sideways smile. He took a step toward her. "As selfish as it may be, I want ye to be mine."

Tears stung her eyes. "Then take me." She gestured toward one of the stalls, her heart pounding in her chest. "Steal my father's horse and grab me as you once did. Ride away and do not stop until we've reached the Highlands!"

He refused her plea with the slightest shake of his head. She covered her face with her hands. What was she to do? She did not want to abandon her family, but she could not imagine a life without Jack in it.

"Where is my Bella?" he whispered, gently tugging her hands away from her face. His soft question inflamed her desire. She wanted so much to be his. She gasped when his fingers stole beneath the edge of her wimple. A soft cry tore from her lips as he pulled, ripping the fabric asunder. At once, his fingers dug into her hair. He crushed his lips against hers. She groaned, wrapping her arms around his neck, fighting to bring their bodies closer, pressing into his hard strength while she savored the taste of him. Then suddenly, he tore his lips from hers. "I love ye," he said, his voice hoarse. He cupped her cheeks between his hands and stroked his thumb across her lips. "Runaway with me," he breathed.

In her heart she already had. She did not doubt that they had been destined to find one another. She could no more deny her heart than she could deny herself water or breath. It pained her to think of hurting Hugh, but his suffering, she knew, would be short-lived. He would marry another—a woman who would look at him and see the sun in her sky, a woman who would love him with her whole heart...something Bella could never do.

For she had given her heart to the man standing in front of her.

Reaching up, she laced her fingers behind Jack's neck. Without a trace of doubt in her heart, she whispered. "I choose love...I choose you."

She glimpsed the light of joy filling his dark eyes the instant before his lips claimed hers. In that moment, unrestrained passion surged through her. She kissed him with all the feeling and warmth that had lay trapped inside her heart for years. She felt as though she were on fire. She savored the heat, and the strength of his embrace. And she knew she had made the right choice—her only choice. Happiness flooded her heart.

Whether Saint Peter or Brother Peter...whether a commoner, highwayman, or rebel—he was one man, her man...Jack MacVie, and she was his Bella.

Chapter Fourteen

When Bella was a little girl, she had gone to market with her mother. Amid the bustle, they'd been separated. Bella had tried to push through the crowd to reach the place where she had last clasped her mother's hand, but the tide of people kept knocking her back. Heart pounding, limbs heavy, she had felt as if she would drown beneath the weight of her terror.

In that moment, tears had flooded her eyes. She had to fight the urge to surrender her quest, to give up and plop to the ground and sob. Clasping to threads of courage, she ceased struggling to get back to where she had been. Instead, she moved with the crowd like a stick tossed in a river that bobbed along with the current. Soon, her fear ebbed, inviting in her intention. New pathways revealed themselves, and then suddenly, she could see her mother ahead of her, her smile beaming like a beacon.

Bella had reached for her mother who seized her hand and pulled her from the swiftly moving river of people. She crushed Bella close and planted kisses all over her face. Then her mother had pulled away slightly and looked down at Bella. "You smart girl," her mother said proudly. "You made your own path, which led to me."

OF ALL THE MEMORIES to flood her thoughts while Bella and Jack walked arm and arm back to the great hall, Bella did not know why she was suddenly reminded of that day at the market with her mother. But she welcomed any distraction from the task ahead—after all, she was moments away from ending her betrothal, declaring her love for a man currently disguised as a monk, and leaving her father to naught but his grief.

But then she realized that her mother was speaking to her...

You can't go back to what was.

You must forge your own path.

Follow your heart.

In that moment, Bella did not doubt that her mother, bold and brave, would have approved of her choice.

"Are ye certain this is what ye want to do?" Jack asked when they reached the door to the great hall.

"Yes, I am," Bella said, her voice strong.

Jack reached for the door.

"Wait," she said and gathered her hair and knotted it at the nape of her neck. Then she squared her shoulders and drew a deep breath. "I am ready now."

Jack swung the door wide. She stepped through. The high dais was empty. She knew her father must have retired to the solar for the night. A pang of regret stabbed her heart as she pictured him there, alone with his misery, but shaking her head, she forced her mind to stay focused.

First, she had to deal with Hugh who was sitting with Quinn and the other monks at one of the long tables. A sad smile tugged at her lips as she watched him throw his head back, his easy laughter ringing out at something the abbot had said. She would always love Hugh. He was her dearest friend, a brother to her soul, but she was never meant to be his wife.

Her stomach twisted as she set off across the room. He looked up when she approached the table. Concern instantly furrowed his brow. He rose. "Bella, what has happened to you?" His fingertips reached out, tucking a wayward lock of her hair behind her ear.

She ignored his question, not wishing to explain why her wimple was in tatters on the stable floor. "May we speak?" she said, her voice low. "In private."

The concern she had glimpsed in his eyes changed to wariness. His shoulders stiffened. Nodding, he gestured for her to go in front of him. Leading the way, she gathered her thoughts, rehearsing how best to tell Hugh that she was in love with another man.

JACK WATCHED AS BELLA turned stiffly on her heel and walked toward the high table. Hugh narrowed his gaze suspiciously on Jack before following her. After they both disappeared behind the screen at the rear of the high dais, Abbot Matthew cleared his throat, drawing Jack's gaze.

"Don't look at me like that," Jack said as he turned away from the abbot's stern eyes.

"Ready yer sword," the older man said dryly. "Ye're a fool if ye think he'll give her up without a fight."

Jack tensed. What if Hugh locked her away in some room or called the Redesdale guard to remove Jack, Quinn, and the abbot from the hall? Bella had reassured him that neither her father nor Hugh would force her to stay.

"Remember who my mother was," she had told him. "My father married for love, and his family supported the matched."

At the time, Jack had bit his tongue, thinking better of pointing out that although her mother had been a commoner, she had also been the daughter of a wealthy merchant; whereas, Jack was a penniless thief.

Jack began to pace back and forth, keeping his gaze trained on the screen. "I should have stolen her when I had the chance."

"I hardly know what you and Lady Redesdale have planned," the abbot began, "and I'm quite certain 'tis better for us all, the less I know. Still, I can quite confidently say that not abducting a lady from her fortress is always the better choice."

Jack stopped and raised his brow at the abbot.

"I must agree with Abbot Matthew on this point," Quinn chimed in.

Jack raked a hand through his shorn hair and renewed his pacing.

After some time, a door slammed. He froze, listening. Soon, heavy footfalls could be heard. Knowing it must be Hugh who approached, Jack glanced at Quinn and said, "Do not interfere." Then he planted his feet wide, keeping his arms lax at his sides.

Jack was the larger man by far. Still, he had resolved not to fight back against Hugh unless he threatened his very life. Moments later, Hugh barreled around the screen and headed toward him with fists clenched, his veins straining against his neck. Jack stiffened, readying his body to absorb the fullness of Hugh's fury. Only steps away now, Hugh pulled his fist back. His nostrils flared. Jack closed his eyes the instant before Hugh's knuckles plowed into his jaw.

Pain shot through Jack's skull. He fell back, landing hard on the rush covered stone floor. Heavy footfalls retreated through the hall, the noise pounding Jack's head.

"Ye deserved that. Didn't ye?"

Jack lifted his eyelids just enough to see Quinn standing above him.

"Aye, that I did," he said, reaching out his hand. "Where did he go?"

Quinn pulled Jack to his feet. "Back the way he came. I presume to try to convince Bella to forget your common, thieving, Scottish hide."

Jack shook his head, then winced, regretting the action.

"Now what do we do?" Quinn asked.

"I do not ken," Jack said, wincing again. "'Tis not every day I steal a lady from her betrothed." He found a seat on one of the benches. "I suppose we wait for Bella."

After what felt like an age to Jack's throbbing head, though it had really been just a matter of minutes, Bella came out from behind the screen with her father and Hugh in tow. Her pain-stricken eyes locked with his.

Jack started toward her, ready to comfort her, but then the doors to the hall burst open. He spun around, his hand grasping for the hilt of his sword, but his fingers gripped only the roughly woven rope around his waist.

"Blast," he cursed under his breath. His only weapon was the dagger strapped to his leg.

Standing tall, he narrowed his gaze on the intruder who stormed into the room with two guards at his side. Straightaway, the Redesdale guard standing on the outskirts of the hall, moved closer, readying their weapons to attack.

Jack could not remember ever encountering the newcomer, but he was a stout man who emanated authority even though he appeared to have fewer than forty years to his credit. His velvet mantle swished about his hips as he turned to scan the hall, his lip curled with open disgust.

"Lord Percy, I did not grant you entry!"

Surprised, Jack glanced back at Isabella's father whose voice had echoed off the ceiling. Lord Redesdale stepped in front of Bella as if shielding her. His eyes flashed with anger. Jack could not believe Lord Redesdale's sudden transformation from frail shadow to mighty defender. Jack swung back around and eyed the intruder. Even he had heard of Lord Percy who was counted among King Edward's favored advisers.

Lord Percy's pale blue eyes narrowed on Lord Redesdale with naked contempt. "You were remiss in not sending word of your daughter's return," he said. "I had to hear from a servant." The word servant flicked off his tongue with disdain as if expelling a disease from his body.

Bella's father stepped forward. "No more remiss than the king not sending me word straight away that she had been attacked on the road."

Lord Percy's eyes narrowed on Lord Redesdale. "How dare you reprimand the king?"

"I will when his folly pertains to my daughter," Lord Redesdale shot back.

Lord Percy gave pause. Then a cocky smile slowly spread his lips wide. "I will not lie, David. Even though you chased away the messenger I sent the last time I called for your support, I came here expecting a vastly different reception. Scottish peasants attacked your daughter. You should be at Berwick Castle as we speak, begging King Edward to retaliate."

Lord Redesdale gestured to Jack. "Brother Peter witnessed the attack. He is convinced those responsible were not peasants, Scottish or otherwise."

Jack stepped forward to show his support for Isabella's father. Still, Lord Percy did not bother to glance his way. He stared hard at Lord Redesdale. "Coward," he spat. "If my daughter was attacked, and her virtue assaulted, I would see those guilty brought to justice!"

"Wait," Jack said, locking eyes with Lord Percy. "I told no one of her near rape." He stalked toward the English lord. "I intentionally left that detail out, thinking it would distress Lord Redesdale unnecessarily." Images of fine swords and tattered clothing flashed in his mind. "It was ye," Jack snarled. "Those were yer men, dressed to look like peasants!"

"Prove it," Lord Percy hissed.

Jack canted his head to the side, eying the lord with deadly intent. "We have several of the attackers' blades in our possession. I've no doubt ye've others just like them in yer armory." Jack lashed out, seizing Lord Percy's tunic in his grasp and slammed his body into the wall. He shot a sidelong glance at Percy's men, but Quinn and the Redesdale guard had them surrounded.

"What of your vows, Brother Peter?" Lord Percy sneered.

A slow smile curved Jack's lips. He pressed his forearm hard against Lord Percy's throat, then leaned close and whispered in his ear. "I'm not a monk." From beneath his robe, Jack produced a dagger, the tip of which he jabbed against Percy's throat. "I'm a thief. My sins are many, and I don't mind adding yer murder to the list."

Lord Percy's eyes narrowed. "You are one of the masked bandits who stole the girl from my men."

Jack shrugged. "Ye aren't in a good position to make accusations."

"Brother Peter, release him!"

Jack glanced over his shoulder. Lord Redesdale stood behind him. His eyes held a feverish gleam. Jack moved aside but kept his dirk at the ready. Lord Redesdale stepped closer. "You ordered your men to attack and rape my daughter?" he said, his voice soft and deadly.

Lord Percy spat on the ground. "She is the daughter of a commoner, a whore whom you have mourned for the last five years when you should have been at court paying homage to your king!"

"My king?" Lord Redesdale said as if he could not believe Lord Percy had dared to speak those words. Jack watched Lord Redesdale's hands curl into tight fists. His chest heaved. "My king!" Lord Redesdale's voice thundered off the high ceilings. He raised his clenched fists in the air, threw his head back and raged. "He killed my wife! My heart," he cried, beating his chest with his own fist. "He is no king!"

Lord Redesdale seized Lord Percy, throwing him to the floor and straddling him. He pulled his fist back and slammed it down, hammering Lord Percy's face again and again. Blood gushed from his nose and mouth and splattered the wall. Lord Redesdale snarled and grabbed Lord Percy's tunic with both hands, lifting his bloodied head off the ground. "I denounce him," Lord Redesdale bellowed in his face. "Do you hear me? I denounce King Edward!" Lord Redesdale's chest heaved as he stood, dragging Percy toward the door. "Get out of my house!"

One of the Redesdale guards grabbed Lord Percy from his lord's hands and tossed him at the feet of his men who lifted him up and carried him from the hall. But before the door closed behind them, Lord Percy shouted, "I will see you drawn and quartered!"

Doom closed in around Isabella, choking the breath from her lungs. She grabbed Jack's hand. "Why did he say that?"

Jack raked his free hand through his hair. "Yer da just denounced King Edward. He's guilty of treason."

"You have to go! Now!"

Isabella whirled around and looked at Hugh who had spoken the rushed words. His hands gripped his hair. Terror had widened his eyes. "You have to go," he said louder, coming toward her. "It will not take Lord Percy long to gather his men. He will come back. You and your father will be arrested. You will be sent to the Tower, and your father will be put to death."

The abbot came forward. "I fear Lord Hugh is correct."

The room started to spin. "Oh God." Her knees gave way, but Hugh caught her.

"Listen to me," Hugh said. "You and your father must run. You cannot delay." Hugh turned to Jack. "Ride north and do not stop until you run out of land. Edward will hunt for them." Hugh looked back to her. Tears stung her eyes. He pulled her close. "I have never imagined life without you. If only I had—" He shook his head. "No, it is too late." He cupped her cheeks. "Be Jack's or someone else's. I don't care. I only care that you live. Promise me you will live!"

She nodded through her tears. "I promise," she said, her heart pounding.

Hugh drew a shaky breath and he stepped back. Then he turned to Jack. "Do not delay." A moment later, Hugh was gone.

Isabella gripped her stomach while she watched Hugh leave her house and her life forever. The room was spinning.

"Do not panic, Bella," Jack said, grabbing her shoulders.

Swallowing down her tears, she nodded, gaining strength from his midnight eyes. She turned to her father.

"I do not regret what I said, Bella." His voice broke. "I spoke the truth. A truth I have swallowed every day since the last time I brought your mother home."

For the first time in years, her father's eyes shone bright and clear. A sob tore from her throat, and she threw her arms around his neck.

"Listen to me, both of ye. 'Tis imperative that we leave now," Jack said.

She looked over her shoulder at Jack. Her eyes narrowed on the vein pulsing at his neck. She nodded, then turned back to her father. She took hold of his hands and brought them to her lips, then she said, "Papa, we must go."

Lord Redesdale's eyes darted about the hall. "But what of our home, our things?"

Jack's fist came down hard on the table behind her, causing her to jump. "They're no longer yers," he growled. "The only possession ye have now is yer life and the lives of yer daughters!"

Bella's heart sank. "Catarina." She grabbed Jack's arm. "My sister's husband, he is not a kind man. There is no telling what he might do!"

Jack squeezed her hand, then turned to Quinn. "Ride to Ravensworth castle and retrieve the Lady Catarina. Ride as if yer very life depends on it, for as sure as the sun will rise, Lady Catarina's life is at stake!"

Quinn nodded and bowed low to Isabella. Lifting his head, his dark eyes smiled up at her. "Fear not, Bella. I will steal your sister away." Without another word, he turned on his heel and raced from the hall.

"Jack," Abbot Matthew said. "We must hurry. We'll leave the wagon and help ourselves to Lord Redesdale's horses."

Jack nodded and grabbed Isabella's elbow, pulling her toward the door.

"Wait," she said.

Jack shook his head. "No more delays, Bella."

"But would not coin be helpful to us?" she asked.

He threw his hands up. "Aye, coin is always helpful."

She pressed a kiss to his lips. Then turned to her father and reached into his pocket, retrieving a key. "I will be right back," she said before racing from the hall and up the stairs to her father's solar. Unlocking the large chest beside his bed, she grabbed several bags of coin and her mother's jewels. Piling everything into a leather satchel, she swung the bag over her shoulder and raced back to the hall.

"We are ready, Jack," she said, barreling into the room.

"Why does everyone keep calling him Jack?" her father said. "I thought his name was Brother Peter."

Isabella grabbed his arm. "I'll explain after we've escaped with our lives!"

Chapter Fifteen

They had left Berwick at a gallop and did not slow their pace until just after dawn when they reached monastic land. The abbot and his monks continued on toward the monastery while Jack, Bella and Lord Redesdale disappeared into the woods.

Beneath the shade of towering pines, Jack expelled a tense breath.

For years, the forest had hidden his family away, allowing their crimes to go unpunished. The trees had been watchful guardians to which he entrusted those he loved most, and would no doubt give them sanctuary one last time.

Patches of mist circled around jutting rocks and wove through the underbrush, painting the earth in white shadow. His appreciative gaze followed the ghostly wisps. Overcome with gratitude, he dropped the reins. While his horse picked its own way toward camp, he wrapped both arms around Bella's waist. She smiled up at him. The morning sun slanted through the leaves, streaking her unbound sable waves with gold. He absently wove his fingers through her hair as he bent his neck back, admiring the tangled, green canopy overhead. Having glimpsed the cold interior of a great fortress, the richness of the forest struck Jack as never before.

Trees like sentinels creaked in the wind, announcing their return as they rode into camp. The pit fire burned bright, and the log seats were fully occupied by three of his brothers, his wee lassies, Rose, and one unexpected visitor. Jack frowned when he met Bishop Lamberton's stern gaze, but an instant later a chorus of girlish squeals erupted as his lassie's raced toward him. He slid from his horse with Bella in his arms and set her down in time to feel the impact of five girls' unabashed delight.

"Jack," they cried.

"Let him breathe, lassies," Rose said, laughing. Jack reached over the girls and gave Rose a hug, but his sister's attention quickly shifted to Bella, which pleased Jack to no end.

"My lady, ye've returned," Rose exclaimed, turning to the woman at his side.

Jack smiled down at Bella who had reached out to embrace his sister. "I never thought I would see you or this place again," Bella said, squeezing Rose tightly.

Rose's eyes welled with happy tears. "Did ye decide to trade yer mighty fortress for my fine cooking?" she's asked, laughing.

"In a manner of speaking," Bella answered hesitantly. She drew away from Rose and took hold of Jack's hand.

"We've much to discuss," Jack said, his voice grave.

Rose arched her brow at him. "What is that supposed to mean?"

"I'll explain," Jack said just as Florie shouldered her way past Moira to hug his leg.

Brows drawn, Ian picked his way around the girls. "Where's Quinn?"

Rory stepped forward. "Aye, Jack, where's Quinn?"

Alec stood beside Rory, his expression impassive.

Before Jack could answer a throat cleared behind him. He turned and looked at Bishop Lamberton.

"Judging by your present company," the bishop said, looking pointedly at Lord Redesdale. "You clearly have much to explain. However, I insist you first remove the robe you wear."

Jack nodded, peeling Florie off his leg. "Forgive me, Bishop. I meant no offense."

Jack disappeared into his hut, emerging minutes later divested of his monastic robes. As he walked back toward the fire, he smiled when he saw Bella's appreciative gaze travel from his tall black boots, past his black hose, to the black tunic belted at his waist. She smiled her approval. He fought the urge to sweep her up into his arms and retreat back to his hut. With regret, he turned from her and looked at her father. "Lord Redesdale, I would like ye to meet Bishop Lamberton; my brothers, Ian, Rory, and Alec; my sister, Rose; and my wee lassies, Moira, Florie, Anna, Mary, and Maggie."

Ian was the first to step forward. He bowed, but Bella's father shook his head. "You need not bow, lad. I am lord of nothing now, except my own conscience. I have, or rather, I will, in due course, be stripped of my titles and wealth."

Jack crossed the glade to his horse and pulled the satchel of coin out of his saddle bags, giving it to Lord Redesdale. "Yer claim of poverty is not entirely true."

"How has this come to be?" Bishop Lamberton asked, his gaze darting between Lord Redesdale and Jack.

Jack cleared his throat. "In short, Lord Redesdale—"

"Please, Jack," Lord Redesdale interrupted. "Call me David."

Jack smiled slightly and nodded. "David has denounced King Edward and is now guilty of treason."

The bishop's eyes widened with surprise. "Then your lives are in danger."

"That is the truth of the matter," David said.

Jack nodded. "We must leave. All of us," he said, raising his voice for his family to hear.

"Wait." Ian grabbed Jack's arm. "What of Quinn? Is he hurt?"

Jack shook his head. "Quinn has journeyed to Ravensworth Castle to retrieve Isabella's sister. Now that Catarina is no longer a lady, Bella and David fear her husband will not honor their marriage."

"Or worse," Bella added.

Brows drawn, Rory asked, "What are the rest of us to do?"

"We must flee," Jack said. "Doubtless Edward has men already searching for our trail." Something pulled at Jack's tunic. He looked down at Florie's smiling face. "Is it time to play yet?" she asked.

He squatted down and motioned for his lassies to come to him. "Nay, my lassies, we cannot play, for we are going on an adventure. And I need all my girls to help Rose with preparations."

"Where will we go?" Rose asked.

"To the Isle of Colonsay," he said. Then he turned to Bella and David. "Our father's people come from there. I am confident we will be welcomed."

"But what of the other children, Jack?" Ian said.

Jack pressed his eyes closed to think. He had not considered the dozens of other children living with various families throughout the countryside who were still reliant on his support.

"We've stolen coin hidden away in the hole," Alec said, his voice flat and his eyes downcast. "That should keep them fed for a while."

BELLA WHIRLED AROUND to face Alec. He must have sensed her gaze because he looked up. She had never seen his face up close. His hair was longer than his brothers and bone straight. His eyes were dark like Jack's, but their emptiness made them appear even darker. A chill crept up her spine as she continued to meet his lonely gaze. Taking a deep breath, she blurted, "Show me the hole."

With a careless shrug, he turned, heading deeper into the woods. She followed. Alec was tall, leanly built with sinewy muscles. There was something sleek in his movements, quiet and effortless.

They followed a narrow path that led to the stream where she, Rose, and the lassies had enjoyed their picnic. Before too long, he stepped off the path toward a patch of dense thicket. "'Tis there," he said, his voice smooth and emotionless.

She stared him hard in the eye. He remained aloof, his face like finely carved wood—beautiful but unchanging. She circled around him and parted the brush and saw the black hole, though she dared not looked down.

Bella arched her brow at him. "This is where you wanted to stick me?"

Alec shrugged. "It seemed a good idea at the time."

Screwing up her courage, she stalked up to him and brushed a lock of black hair from his eyes. Despite his shield of impassivity, she could feel his power as one feels the strength of a caged animal. Then, she remembered Rose confessing that he had the sight.

Suddenly, she felt as if a blaze of heat passed from his body into hers. And for a moment, she felt his pain. "You feel nothing to keep from feeling everything," she blurted.

His expression never altered. "Let's go," he said. Then without another word, he turned around and headed back toward camp.

Her legs trembled as she followed behind his sleek body, and she remembered Rose telling her that she had a special place for Alec in her heart.

Now Bella understood why.

There was something inside Alec that he hid behind his cool indifference, something powerful and broken.

Back at camp a bustle of activity was underway. She crossed to where her father stood. "Are you well, Papa? You seem confused."

He smiled, crinkling his pale green eyes. "I'm not confused, perhaps a trifle overwhelmed. As far as I can tell, Rose and Jack's lassies are coming with us, but Jack and Bishop Lamberton appear to disagree on whether or not his brothers should come."

Bella looked across the glade to where Jack and the bishop stood away from the others. She could see the strain on Jack's face. Her heart broke for him. She knew all too well the pain of a family divided and lost. Chewing on her lip, she considered crossing the glade and intruding upon their conversation, but then her father's hand clasped hers. She met his gaze.

"I see your concern, my dear," her father said gently. "But remember, Bishop Lamberton is one of the most powerful men in Scotland. Do not forget yourself."

She expelled a slow breath. "You're right, Papa."

He patted her hand tenderly. "Do not worry, my dear. Remember, hope for a heart-full—"

She threw her arms around her father's neck. "And never take for granted a mouthful," she finished for him. Drawing back slightly, she met his gaze. "You've come back to me, Papa."

He smiled through his tears. "I have, Bella." His brow drew together with concern. "I'm just sorry that my awakening has come at the cost of my daughters' titles."

Bella lifted her shoulders. "I was already planning on giving up my title." Her thoughts turned to her sister. "Catarina, I'm certain, had no such plan, but my heart tells me to trust Quinn. He will save her."

Her father took a deep breath. "Despite what your sister may believe, she deserves so much more than Lord Ravensworth. His heart is cruel. She may have tried to argue otherwise, but you can see his hardness in his eyes. I pray that Quinn is able to convince her to leave Ravensworth Castle."

A smile curved Bella's lips as she shifted her gaze to Jack who was still speaking with the bishop. "I do not believe that will be a problem. The MacVie men can be very persuasive."

Chapter Sixteen

Five years ago, Jack's parents and youngest sister had been slaughtered on the streets of Berwick—their only crime had been being born on Scottish soil. Grief, quiet but relentless, lived on in his heart.

"You know what you must do," the bishop said, drawing Jack's thoughts back to the present.

Jack raked his fingers through his hair. "I cannot divide my family."

"Do you think they will be safer with you?" Bishop Lamberton rested his hand on Jack's shoulder. "You are on the run, Jack. There will be a price on your head. But your brothers are still unknown, traceless." The bishop paused, drawing a deep breath. "Damn it, Jack, Scotland still needs The Saints!"

Jack knew The Saints were essential to the bishop's work. He was building an army of secret rebels, and the MacVie men were at the heart of it all. Jack looked to where his brothers stood listening to Jack and Bishop Lamberton's debate. They were men grown, even Ian. Mayhap the reason why Jack could not decide the next best course of action was because it was not his decision to make. "They must choose for themselves," he said, meeting Rory's earnest gaze.

Rory drew close. "The cause is in my blood. I want to stay and be useful to the bishop. I want to fight for Scotland!"

Jack closed his eyes against the tightening in his chest. Instinct bade he fight to keep his family together. Still, at two and twenty, Rory was a man. He met Rory's pale blue gaze. "Stick to the code, Brother. Be bold, not reckless."

"To the former, ye have my word," Rory vowed. Then a smile upturned the corner of his mouth. "To the latter, I will do my best." Then he looked Jack hard in the eye. "Be careful, Jack. *Alba gu bràth*, Scotland Forever!"

Jack clamped his hand on Rory's shoulder. "*Alba gu bràth*!"

Then Jack crossed the glade to where Alec had moved, standing on his own. For several moments, Jack waited for Alec to look at him or speak his choice, but his younger brother remained silent, his gaze fixed on the ground.

"Have ye seen what lies ahead?" Jack asked, his chest tightening for fear of what his brother might say.

"I've seen yer future. 'Tis clear and light, but only if ye ride hard."

Jack swallowed hard. "What of yerself and the others?"

Alec shook his head slightly. "Our futures are in shadow, even Rose's. The only certitude I can give ye, is that our paths must now diverge."

Emotion welling deep within his soul, Jack seized Alec, pulling him into a fierce hug. When he drew away, he looked Alec hard in the eye. "Make yer way to Colonsay one day."

Urgency suddenly filled Alec's empty gaze. "Ride hard!"

Jack pulled away and was startled by the rare glimpse of emotion in his brother's gaze. But an instant later, Alec's black eyes, once again, became as cool and impassive as a starless night sky.

Taking a deep breath, Jack stepped back and looked to his youngest brother who was sitting on the ground, letting Moira braid his long, tangled red hair.

"What say ye?" Jack said, then held his breath, not wanting to say goodbye to another of his siblings.

Ian looked up at Jack. "Bishop Lamberton is right. Ye're an outlaw now and so are Bella and David. Ye cannot run with five wee ones. *I* will take Rose and the lassies to Colonsay. We strike out on our own."

Jack expelled the breath he'd been holding. He placed his hand on his youngest brother's wide shoulder. "Thank ye, Ian."

Bishop Lamberton stepped forward then, drawing Jack's gaze. "I will ensure the other children are cared for, which settles matters." Then a warning crept into the bishop's voice. "You can delay no longer. You must put some distance between you and Edward's soldiers."

Jack reached out clasped the bishop's offered hand. "Thank ye for everything."

Bishop Lamberton smiled. "You have given more than your share to the cause, Jack. Now is your chance to claim that peaceful life I know you dream about when you think no one is watching."

With a full heart, Jack wrapped his arm around Bella's waist. "I am already there." He felt himself sinking into the deep green sea of her eyes. "Bella," he breathed. "Are ye ready to win this day and ride to freedom?"

She wrapped her arms around his neck. "Freedom isn't won, Jack. It's stolen." A glint of excitement lit her gaze. "Let's ride!"

BELLA'S SOUL SOARED to the tops of the surrounding mountains. She breathed the fresh, crisp air and felt its elusive truth, untamed, unpredictable—and now, for the first time, so was she.

Nudging her horse in the flanks, she skirted around jagged rocks and climbed rugged, jutting slopes. With courage in her heart, she watched storm clouds gather, clinging to the mountaintops. A crack of lightning sliced the sky, unleashing torrents of heavy rain, but she did not shrink from the downpour. She threw her head back and cried out as wild as any creature ever to cross mountain or moor.

Jack raced alongside her, adding to her sense of wonderment. Never had she felt so complete.

Glancing back, she looked to her father who was huddled beneath his cape. Still, a smile stretched his face wide. Witnessing his irrepressible joy, her heart swelled. He had been delivered up from his grief. This was a new world, one far from pain.

After a while, the dark clouds scattered, releasing the sun's warmth and light. The road wound around craggy boulders and small forests of Scotch pine and then straightened, running alongside a large field left to fallow. At its edge, they passed a black smith's forge. Black plumes of smoke coiled out from rooftop vents. Further down they came to a village green with a small, stone kirk at its center. Few people milled about the sleepy hamlet, but those who were crossing the green or bringing wheat to the mill beyond the kirk stopped and stared at Bella.

"Yer clothes are too rich," Jack said, under his breath. "Yer da's, too."

She looked down at her sodden yet fine tunic with its intricate embroidery and golden threads. Bella scanned the village. "Where is the tailor?"

Jack chuckled. "There is no tailor, not for miles and miles. Bella, most people make their own clothes."

She blushed while at the same time squaring her shoulders. "Then, I must learn."

"I think that a fine idea," Jack said approvingly. "But it does not solve our immediate problem. Yer tunic invites suspicion."

"True," she said, looking about. Then she spied a young woman with a basket of laundry in her arms passing between two huts. When she disappeared from view, she looked at Jack. "Wait for me at the outskirts of the village."

Jack and her father exchanged skeptical glances. "What are you planning to do?" David asked.

"Just go," she urged. When neither man moved, she scowled. "Fine, I will go." She nudged her horse forward, following the path taken by the girl. After a brief while, Bella spotted her near the edge of a field laying out clothes on top of tall grasses. Keeping back, she waited until the girl had emptied her basket. The girl stood for a moment, her gaze upturned to the sun.

Her heart started to race when the girl turned, retreating back the way she'd come. "Now," she said to herself. Holding her breath, Bella slid from her horse and darted to the edge of the field. As quickly as she could, she snatched a kirtle and tunic for herself and a pair of hose and a tunic for her father. With a shaky hand, she dropped several coins on top of an apron spread out in the fleeting sunshine. Her heart pounded as she ran back to her horse. Shoving the items into her satchel, she pulled herself up into her saddle and made a dash for the road.

"Let's ride," she shouted, passing Jack and her father. They quickly followed.

"What did ye do?" Jack asked, bringing his horse alongside hers.

"I purchased some new clothing," she said with a wink.

He raised a brow at her. "Don't ye mean to say that ye stole some new clothing?"

She grinned widely. "I believe I left her enough coin to buy the whole village, should she desire. So, even though I didn't ask, I'll stand by my claim that the exchange was, indeed, a purchase."

Jack laughed. The rich sound enveloped her. She reached across the space between them, and he stretched his hand out. Their fingertips touched, sending heat coursing through her body. She had never felt so alive.

After changing horses at the next small village, they continued their race. The countryside was beautiful, lush with rolling hills painted in verdant spring colors. But it was not the distant mountains or rolling moorland that kept drawing her gaze. Jack's rugged allure left her breathless and full of need. A sweet ache was building inside her, an ache that brought both pleasure and pain. It left her hungry for Jack's touch. And no gentle caress would do. She wanted to feel the strength of his hands on her body. She wanted him to possess her, body and soul.

Every moment not spent in his arms was agony. And judging by the intense fire she glimpsed in his ebony gaze, he was growing as impatient as she to find accommodations for the night.

When the sun dipped below the horizon, they, at last, came upon another village. Leaving Bella and David at the edge of the village green, Jack went to speak with the proprietor of a bustling alehouse.

"Thank goodness," David said, meeting Bella's gaze. "For the first time in years, my limbs are filled with vigor. Still, I do not believe I am quite ready to sleep out of doors."

"My thinking has been the same," Bella claimed, although sleep was certainly not what she had on her mind. Still, she was not going to tell her father that Jack's strong hands and broad shoulders had been the true occupants of her thoughts.

"Luck is on our side," Jack said when he returned. "We've the last two rooms."

A wave of relief passed over her father's face the instant before his brows drew together with concern. "Prepare yourself, daughter. Our room is sure to offer little by way of comfort."

Bella's eyes flashed wide. The last thing she wanted was to share a room with her father.

Jack cleared his throat. "David, ye're bedding down on yer own."

Bella's heart started to pound. She met Jack's hot gaze.

"But where do you intend to sleep?" David asked Jack, and then his breath caught as his gaze darted between Jack and Bella. "Surely, you do not intend to share a room with my daughter."

Jack drew back a step. "That is exactly my intention." He threw his hands out. "But do not fash yerself. First, I plan to wed her."

Bella's heart raced. She could not draw breath.

The heat in his gaze gave way to tenderness. "That is...if ye'll have me," he said, his voice soft and low. He reached out and grazed the backs of his fingers down her cheek. "My Bella," he whispered.

She threw her arms around his neck. "Nothing could make me happier." But then, remembering her father, she stiffened and drew away. "Papa?" she said, her eyes pleading for him to understand her heart.

A scowl furrowed her father's brow. In that moment, he was every bit Lord Redesdale; the relieved and spirited David had vanished. "Of all the offensive, improper...." His voice trailed off. He cast his gaze to the ground, expelling a long breath. When he looked at her once more, his face had softened.

David had returned.

He stepped forward and cupped her cheek. "It seems my new life demands I relinquish control, a daunting but not unwelcome task. I have no qualms with the match if this is where your heart lies. He has proved himself to be an intelligent man of great heart. More than that, he clearly loves you." He turned his gaze to Jack. "I could ask nothing more for my Bella." Then his smile faded. "But forgive me for saying so, you do already have a lot of children."

Bella laughed outright. "Jack's lassies are not of his body, Papa. They are simply in his charge." Once more her father appeared confused. She pressed a kiss to his cheek. "They are orphans, exiled after the massacre. Jack saved them."

Warmth flooded David's gaze. "You are, indeed, a noble man, Jack MacVie." He smiled at Bella. "You have my blessing."

Their wedding was perfect with none of the pomp and frivolities of noble custom; they did not even stand for Mass. She wore her stolen dress of homespun wool. Jack had made her a crown of wildflowers, which he laid on her unbound hair. On her father's arm, she walked the short length of the alehouse common room and stood in front of the local priest who, as fortune would have it, had been at one of the tables enjoying a mug of ale. In just a few short minutes, they were married, and she did not think she could have waited a minute more. The look of hunger in Jack's eyes was a mirror of her own desire.

"Shall we feast?" David said, proudly pointing to a large spread of baked apples, stewed chestnuts, meat pies, bannock and ale.

God above forgive her, but the last thing she wanted at that moment was to sit down and eat. She looked at Jack. The pulse at his neck raced. Her feet pointed toward the stairs. His fists clenched and unclenched at his sides. Finally, she forced a smile to her lips and was about to thank her father and sit down when an old woman in a voluminous black cloak drew near.

"Can't ye see they're not hungry," the woman said to David. "At least not for food." She turned and winked at Bella. She had soft, kind gray eyes and silvery hair pulled back from her face, which was creased with age. She sat down next to David. "As for me, well, it has been a good while since I sat down to such a feast." She reached for one of the small pies and took a bite.

"Mmm, eel...delicious," she mumbled as she chewed. Then she washed it down with a sip of ale. "Didn't they have pigeon?" she asked.

Bella pressed her lips together to keep from laughing at the appalled look on father's face. First giving Bella a sly smile, the old woman then turned back to David. "Surely, you were young once," she said with a wink.

David's expression softened. "Would you believe that I was?"

The old woman smiled. "I would. And I also believe you were once truly loved by a woman."

A distant look clouded her father's eyes, and a slight smile curved his lips. "Indeed, I was," he whispered. Leaning back in his chair, he looked up at Bella. "I wish you both every happiness," he said softly.

Tears stung Bella's eyes. "Are you certain, Papa?"

David nodded. "I will be fine." Then he turned to the old woman at his side. "What is your name?"

"Gertrude," she replied.

"It is a pleasure to meet you," David said before turning back to Bella. "Gertrude will keep me company."

"Thank you, Papa," Bella whispered.

With a dip of his head to her father, Jack turned and led her upstairs. Her heart raced as he opened the door to their room. Stepping inside, she quickly scanned the cramped space. Her gaze settled on the narrow bed. Then the rest of the room was forgotten.

The door slammed behind her. She whirled around and opened her arms just as Jack reached for her. Pulling the flower crown from her head, he sent it soaring across the room. Then his fingers dug into her hair, and, at last, he kissed her with all the strength and passion her soul had craved.

His tongue dove between her lips, releasing the fullness of her hunger. His hands cupped her cheeks and then her neck and then caressed down her shoulders. He tore his lips away. His black eyes were hard and heavy. He grabbed her tunic and yanked it over her head. Her kirtle quickly followed. She was bare to his midnight eyes. He drew a shaky breath and ran a finger slowly down her breastbone to her navel and then, slower still, sweeping his fingers across the curls at the apex of her thighs. Her legs trembled. An agonizing ache shuddered through her. Her body tingled wherever he touched. He stepped back and jerked free from his clothes. Her gaze raked over the hard lines of his chest and stomach. His smell surrounded her, drawing her in.

She reached out and grazed the crisp, black hair fanning across his chest. His breathing quickened, and his skin shone with sweat. She leaned close and pressed her lips to the hollow of his neck, savoring the salty taste of his skin. With a groan, he pulled her against him. Then he bent his head and breathed hot currents of air over her hardened nipples. She cried out when his teeth lightly bit down, drawing first one sensitive peak into his mouth and then the other.

Moving his lips slowly down her stomach, his fingers pressed her thighs apart. He sank to his knees, gripped her buttocks and pulled the wet heat of her to his lips. She threw her head back and cried out as fire, hot and searing, coursed through her. Her breath hitched. She whimpered. Agonizing need begged her hips to tilt into his kiss.

When he pulled away, cool air teased her desire. He clasped her close and laid her on the bed. Then he covered her with his full weight, kissing her, fueling the flames of her yearning. He grasped her hips and, slowly, he entered her. Her fingers bit into his shoulders. She flung her head back, arching her chest while she writhed beneath his muscular strength. He thrust deeper, and deeper still, harder and harder. She reached, climbing, soaring until at last, her body seized. She shuddered around him as wave after wave of sweet relief coursed through her.

Bella lay in Jack's embrace. His fingertips grazed the length of her spine. She shivered and looked up at him through bleary eyes and smiled. "You are many things, Jack MacVie, and now you can add being the love of my life to the list."

Then her lids opened wide. She sat up. "Something just occurred to me."

He rolled over onto his back and laced his fingers behind his head. "Aye? And what is that?"

She leaned out of bed and scooped her tunic off the floor. "In truth, I did take this without asking, which means I stole it."

He smiled. "But we both already knew that."

She started to laugh.

"What's so funny?" he asked.

"You and I are married."

He frowned. "Although I do not see the humor in that, we are, indeed, married. There's an alehouse full of witnesses able to attest to that fact."

She could not contain her laughter.

"Are ye going to tell me what ye find so amusing, wife?"

She hiccupped and nodded. Reaching her arms around his neck, she said, "It just occurred to me that I am now a thief, an outlaw, a commoner, and a Scotswoman. You and I are now a perfect match."

He smiled and pulled her close. Then he rolled over, pushing her back onto the bed. "I hope this does not disappoint ye, but I believe my thieving days are over...In truth, ye married a fisherman."

"I think that fine," she said, reaching up to cup his cheek. She lost herself in his midnight gaze.

Her heart swelled thinking of the unknown road ahead of her. Once upon a time, she had felt trapped in a cage of sorrow. Her future held nothing but loveless companionship and despair. But now, her arms were full. She could breathe freely. Her heart knew hope.

She met Jack's gaze. "I love you," she said simply.

His eyes were filled with warmth. "I've loved ye since the moment I first dried yer tears and soothed ye to sleep in my arms."

She licked her lips and brought her mouth a breath from his. "I hope you don't have any aspirations for sleep this night."

He kissed her long and hard. "Like our life together, this night has just begun." A playful smile curved his lips. "And it will be long and full of surprises."

Pulling her beneath him, his lips began to journey over her body. Taking his time, he showed every inch of her the love and passion her soul had always craved.

Chapter Seventeen
Epilogue

Jack gripped his fishing boat and bent low, pressing his shoulder into the stern. "Alright, lads, put yer backs into it," he called to Ian and David who flanked the boat on either side. They trudged forward, the hull carving into the sand. Icy water lapped Jack's calves until the waves receded, swallowing the shore out from beneath his feet. A moment later, the surf barreled forward, churning once more around his legs. This dance continued until they had moved the boat beyond the ocean's hungry reach.

He straightened and stretched his back, then wiped at the beads of sweat on his forehead with the back of his hand. "Are ye well?" he said, sitting down on the sand next to David who was trying to catch his breath. David's white hair stood on end in the wind. Dirt and dried salt streaked his ruddy face.

He looked at Jack warmly. "I would be lying if I said that I've never felt happier. However, if I cannot have my Annunziatta at my side, then I can tell you with the greatest sincerity, there is no place I would rather be."

Jack smiled and fell back in the sand. The hot summer sun had begun to dip behind the horizon, making way for cool evening breezes, which poured off the waves. The music of the calm ocean matched the beat of his heart.

"Look," Ian called. "Here they come."

Jack sat up. His lassies splashed through the ebbing waves while Bella and Rose walked a little behind, both with deep baskets strapped to their backs to carry the day's catch back to their croft. A slow smile curved Jack's lips as he watched Bella approach. Water lapped her bare feet. The wind whipped her tunic against one side of her body, hugging her curves. His gaze traced along the outline of her sleek waist and the flare of her hip. Her hair, streaked with pale gold, fanned out behind her, lifting and tangling in the salty air.

Her eyes locked with his. A smile, sweet and sensual, curved her lips as she drew closer. When she reached his side, she sank to her knees and pulled the basket from her shoulders. Then she lay her head on his chest. He closed his eyes and savored the feel of her, more precious to him than anything he could have ever imagined. He wrapped his arm around her and stroked her hair.

She raised her head and looked at him, her pale green eyes luminescent next to her skin, now deeply tanned by the sun. He grazed his fingers down her soft cheek and throat, then slowly over her shoulder. He frowned when he noticed a hole in the sleeve of her tunic. He absently picked at the frayed threads.

"Do ye miss yer life the way it was?" he said. "Yer fine tunics and servants."

Her eyes widened for an instant and then grew serious. She cupped his cheeks between her hands. "You listen to me, Jack MacVie. All I want is you." She sat up and pointed to Rose and the lassies trying to get as close to the waves as they could without getting wet. "And them," she said, laughing. Then she jumped to her feet and spread her arms wide, smiling up at the heavens. "And Colonsay," she cried. "Sandy shores, crashing waves, Jura's mountains in the distance." She plunked down in the sand once more and wrapped her arms around his neck, pulling him to lay back on the sand.

"Look," she cried. He followed her outstretched arm, pointing to the sky at a golden eagle soaring into the clouds. Then she touched his cheek, drawing his gaze. Her warm breath caressed his skin. "Thank you," she whispered.

"For what?" he asked, his voice low.

"For giving me a wonderful life."

Jack closed his eyes, held his beautiful wife close, and listened to the ocean's song.

For so long, he had dreamed of returning to life as a fisherman. But never could he have imagined that his own adventures would end on the very isle from where his family once hailed.

In that moment, his mind turned to his siblings. His brow drew together when he thought about Quinn.

Would his brother reach Catarina in time? Would Bella's sister trust Quinn enough to leave her home? His nostrils flared as worry washed over him.

And what about Rory and Alec?

They had chosen to remain a part of Bishop Lamberton's secret rebel army. Jack did not doubt that the bishop had ambitious plans for his brothers. But now, he wouldn't be there to watch out for them.

Jack lifted his head and glanced at where Rose and Ian stood together watching the lassie's play. At least, Jack could still keep an eye on them. But then he remembered Alec's words. He had said that Ian and Rose's futures were also cast in shadow.

"Jack," Bella said, her voice laced with concern.

He glanced down at her.

Brows drawn, she sat up. "You're scowling suddenly."

He expelled a long breath.

She looked at him knowingly. "You were fretting again."

He nodded.

She sat up. "You're a wanted man now. I've no doubt your likeness as well as my own and my father's is hanging in every tavern from London to Berwick and beyond with a handsome bounty on our heads. Your distance is all you can do now to keep them safe."

He took another deep breath. "I ken ye're right."

She lay back down, nestling into his chest. "You're the eldest brother. You will always worry. I, too, worry for Catarina."

"What do ye do when the worry for yer sister sets in?"

She smiled up at him. "I remember that Quinn MacVie is on his way to rescue her." Her smile widened. She pressed a kiss to his chest. "I know from experience that MacVie men will stop at nothing to rescue a lady in danger, even when their first intention is to rob her." She sat up and met his gaze. "I love you so much, Jack." A gentle smile curved her lips. "Even though you first planned to attack my carriage and steal my worldly possessions."

He chuckled. "I'm happy to have relinquished St Peter's black mask for a fishing net."

She cupped his cheek. "You may no longer be one of Scotland's secret rebels, but you will always be the thief of my heart."

"And ye," he said, his voice low and husky. "Will always be my princess."

The End

QUINN: A SCOTTISH OUTLAW

Does Quinn rescue Bella's sister, Catarina, in time? Read their
story next

An excerpt from Quinn: A Scottish Outlaw

QUINN MACVIE NEVER ran his horse ragged, and he'd
berate any man who did. But if he had to choose between the
well-being of a horse or that of a woman—he would pick the
woman every time.

"Open the doors," Quinn shouted outside the stables of
what might have been a bustling village were it not the middle
of the night. The swollen moon cast cool light across the barren
village green and narrow road. He knocked again on the worn
wooden door. Surely, someone slept within. A flicker of
candlelight across the road snaked his gaze toward one of the
small cottages. He glimpsed a shadowed face the instant before
a flap of hide fell back in place over the cottage window,

146

concealing its occupant from view. At least someone had heard his plea. Now, if only the stable master would stir.

"Wake Up. I need a horse," Quinn yelled, emphasizing each word with a hammer of his fist upon the door.

Still, aid did not arrive. With a growl, he pounded the door harder, again and again, until at last he heard the bar slide away. He stepped back as the doors swung wide. Orange lantern light fell upon a grizzly looking man with thick brows, a wide, flat nose and long, tangled brown hair. A line of spittle that had dried to his chin and his glazed eyes proved that Quinn had, indeed, dragged the man from a sound sleep, and judging by his deep scowl, he was not at all pleased. Holding his lantern high, the man glared at Quinn.

"What the devil are ye..." His raspy voice trailed off, and his eyes widened as he looked Quinn over.

Pulling his weary mount behind him, Quinn barreled into the stables, his long, black robe swirling about his feet. Inside, the air smelled of fresh-cut hay. Quinn grunted his approval. "I need a horse," he said, turning back to look at the stable master.

"Forgive me, Brother," he said, making the sign of the cross. "I did not expect to find a monk beating down my door at this hour. 'Tis after midnight. I thought to find a lad new to his breeches and too far into his cups."

"I need a horse," Quinn repeated. He hadn't time for conversation. Promises had been made. A life was at stake. "I've pushed this beast too hard." He tossed the man his reins.

Frowning, the man slipped the handle of his lantern on a nearby hook before his attention turned to the mare. He stroked her muzzle. "Ye're a pretty lass," he said, revealing a row of square, yellow teeth when he smiled. "But a tired one to be sure." He looked beyond the mare to Quinn. "She's young and will recover," he said, wiping at the white foam that had gathered on the horse's bit.

Nodding his approval, Quinn gestured to the line of stalls stretching out behind them into darkness. "Another mount and hurry. 'Tis a matter of great urgency."

Without hesitation, the man hastened to the nearest stall. "I'm called Adam MacDonough," he said, fumbling with the latch. "Remember my name in yer prayers. I wouldn't deny a man of God aid, and neither would my lord. He wouldn't dare." Adam opened the gate, then quitted the stall a moment later with a white, speckled mare in tow. "I will pray for yer quest, Brother," he said while saddling the horse. "What's yer saint's name?"

"Augustine," Quinn bit out, rubbing the back of his neck while he waited impatiently for the man to finish.

Adam's straggly hair swept the dirt floor as he leaned down and tightened the cinch before he straightened and handed the reins to Quinn. "Brother Augustine, will ye say a blessing for me?"

Quinn looked away from the disheveled man's imploring gaze. He had no wish to add to his list of sins by committing such a blatant blasphemy. It was one thing to dress the part of a monk. Surely, God would turn a blind eye to a simple disguise. But to perform a blessing in His name—even Quinn had to draw the line somewhere. Keeping silent, he gathered his long robe and swung up into the saddle. Wishing to at least offer Adam his thanks, he glanced down, but the stable master's gaze had fixed on the hilt of the large dirk sticking out of Quinn's boot. Quinn quickly dropped the voluminous folds of his black robe in place, hiding the weapon from view. "'Tis my soul that's in jeopardy. Pray for me," Quinn hissed and tossed a handful of coin on the ground. "To appease the nobleman who owns this beast." Then Quinn turned his horse away from the startled man and drove his heels into the mare's flanks, racing back out into the night.

For five years, Quinn had routinely broken one of the ten commandments—Thou shall not steal. He was a thief, robbing English nobles on the road north into Scotland alongside his four brothers. But the MacVie brothers were not hell bent on riches and wealth. They had become highwaymen to fight against the tyranny of King Edward of England, giving their gains to a cause greater than themselves, the righteous call of Scottish sovereignty. Over the years, Quinn had stolen chests of coin, jewels, fine tapestries, costly robes, anything that might fetch a price. Now, once again, he was bent low over a saddle in pursuit of a prize, but what he had agreed to steal was unlike any plunder he had stolen before. He rode north through Scotland, urging his horse to race faster, not in pursuit of gold or jewels. He was after something infinitely more valuable. He was after a woman, an English woman, Lady Catarina Ravensworth to be exact.

What few knew at that moment was that Lady Catarina's father, Lord David Redesdale, had just committed treason only hours before. But word would spread and soon everyone would know, including King Edward. If caught, David would be drawn and quartered for his crimes, but, luckily for David, he and his youngest daughter, Bella, had fled from their fortress in England with Quinn's older brother, Jack, at their side. Now outlaws on the run, they would have to move fast to escape the violent wrath of King Edward, but if anyone could lead David and Bella to safety, it was Jack. However, just before they left, Bella expressed grave concern for her sister's well-being. She told Jack and Quinn that her sister was wed to a cruel English lord who would punish Catarina for her father's disgrace.

The thought of Lord Henry Ravensworth drove Quinn to push his horse harder. There was nothing more loathsome than a man willing to raise his fist against a woman or child. Judging by Bella's distress, Quinn had surmised her brother-in-law to be just that sort of man. Now it was up to Quinn to steal Catarina away before news of David's treason reached Lord Ravensworth.

Quinn had ridden along the coast for some hours when at last the horizon began to brighten. He tugged on the reins, bringing his horse to a halt and inhaled the pungent scent of low tide. Up ahead, the torch fire of Ravensworth Castle blazed against the waning night sky. He slid from his horse and stroked a soothing hand down his horse's muzzle. It would only encourage suspicion were he to arrive at Ravensworth with a winded beast. He looked down at his black robe, the very robe he had worn to gain entry the morning before into the Redesdale fortress. As a humble monk, he would walk the remainder of the journey, and by the time he neared the gate, the sea should be slashed with the golds and pinks of dawn. A slight smile curved his lips. Brother Augustine would have no trouble gaining entry into Ravensworth Castle. Then his smile vanished. Leaving the castle with the lady of the keep—now that was the real challenge.

Go to http://lilybaldwinromance to read *Quinn: A Scottish Outlaw.*
Thank you for choosing the Highland Outlaws Series!
May you always feel the pulse of the Highlands in your heart.
Hugs,
Lily Baldwin

Made in the USA
Monee, IL
11 May 2022